NORSE MYTHOLOGY LEGENDS

EPIC STORIES, QUESTS, MYTHS & MORE FROM THE MOST POWERFUL CHARACTERS, GODS, GODDESSES & HEROES OF NORSE & VIKING FOLKLORE

HISTORY BROUGHT ALIVE

© Copyright 2022 - All rights reserved.

The content contained within this book may not be reproduced, duplicated, or transmitted without direct written permission from the author or the publisher.

Under no circumstances will any blame or legal responsibility be held against the publisher, or author, for any damages, reparation, or monetary loss due to the information contained within this book, either directly or indirectly.

<u>Legal Notice:</u>

This book is copyright protected. It is only for personal use. You cannot amend, distribute, sell, use, quote, or paraphrase any part, or the content within this book, without the consent of the author or publisher.

<u>Disclaimer Notice:</u>

Please note the information contained within this document is for educational and entertainment purposes only. All effort has been executed to present accurate, up-to-date, reliable, complete information. No warranties of any kind are declared or implied. Readers acknowledge that the author is not engaged in the rendering of legal, financial, medical, or professional advice. The content within this book has been derived from various sources. Please consult a licensed professional before attempting any techniques outlined in this book.

By reading this document, the reader agrees that under no circumstances is the author responsible for any losses, direct or indirect, that are incurred as a result of the use of the information contained within this document, including, but not limited to, errors, omissions, or inaccuracies.

FREE BONUS FROM HBA: EBOOK BUNDLE

Greetings!

First of all, thank you for reading our books. As fellow passionate readers of History and Mythology, we aim to create the very best books for our readers.

Now, we invite you to join our VIP list. As a welcome gift, we offer the History & Mythology Ebook Bundle below for free. Plus you can be the first to receive new books and exclusives! Remember it's 100% free to join.

Simply scan the QR code to join.

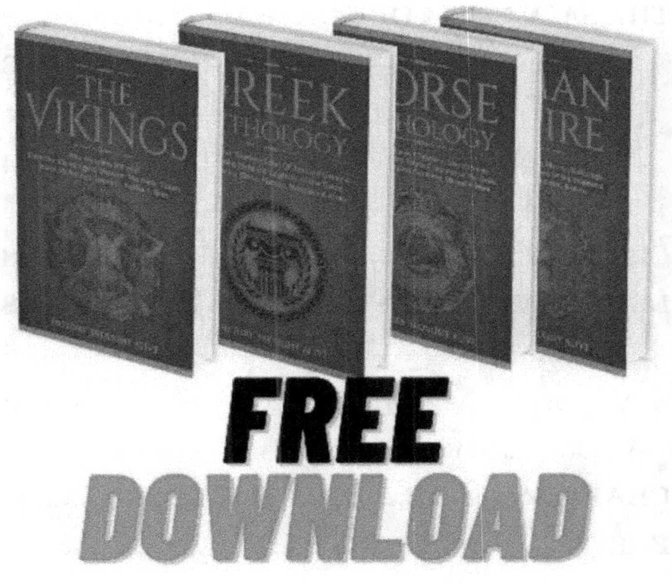

CONTENTS

INTRODUCTION

Fear not death for the hour of your doom is set and none may escape it.

Norse mythology today is usually told on a myth by myth basis, or it is embellished to make a hit Netflix show. A lot of those shows are really well done, and sometimes you can stumble on a telling of the mythology in chronological order. There is just one thing missing from it all.

Often, if people try to research specific figures in Norse mythology, there are a few conflicting stories. You click from site to site or read from book to book. Because of that, it's hard to get closer to those figures or what qualities they canonically present.

At History Brought Alive, we are a team of enthusiasts from all walks of life who specialize in history and mythology. We are fascinated by beliefs, customs, traditions, and even myths that have shaped our society. Through the collective passion that we put into our books and YouTube channel, we try to make elements of history and diverse cultures more accessible. As a collective, we have put forth works like *Mythology of Mesopotamia, Ancient Egypt, Native American History*, and many, many more. Why do we do this? It is not only because we are enthusiasts, but this is because we believe that history and mythology should be accessed by everyone. This means that we believe in having some fun while you learn. Everyone is going to be a little curious, and the density of a lot of the available research can be daunting. What about the casual, curious party? Everyone should get to learn about subjects as fantastical as these. Learning is and should be fun, so we do our best to make sure our information is as engaging as possible. We'll also give you the means to learn at your own pace and pursue your own research. There is no better way to do that than by giving you those stories in an easy-to-read and digestible format.

By reading this book, you will learn:

- A brief history of Norse mythology as the stories that were written as the Viking age faded away. How close were we to losing it all? How did it stay alive, and is it all just myths still or an active belief system today?

- A brief and yet detailed telling of

creation, as it was told by Norse mythology.

- You will get an overview of who the Norse characters were, their prized possessions, what their names mean today, and their family tree. Then, we will tell myths tied to that figure from the tragic to the comedic.

- We can't mention creation without mentioning destruction. We will cover the biggest event in Norse mythology, Ragnarök.

- Finally, we will list how Norse mythology has thrived in pop culture. The shows, movies, video games, and more that keep our favorite gods alive.

Norse mythology, as you will learn, was carried for centuries as an oral tradition. Some deliveries of these stories were grand while some of them were aimed to be cautionary tales.

That is how this book will deliver those stories to you—as if you were being charged with carrying on a piece of mythology to the next generation of listening ears.

That means there will be no direct tellings of things you've heard before. Everyone can tell you a story but seldom can make you actually feel the emotions of the myths. Again, we are major enthusiasts of the subjects we love.

This also means you will not have to trade one eye, impale yourself with your trusted spear, and hang yourself from Yggdrasil to drink from Mimir's well. You just have to read this book. You were like Odin and we were your ravens who collected the stories for you.

So, take your place upon your own Hlidskjalf, and let's get ready to meet the characters of

Norse mythology!

CHAPTER 1
THE SALVATION OF
NORSE MYTHOLOGY

Norse mythology is one of the more fascinating subjects to discuss. It's a subject that could be told in terms of lavish, bombastic tellings of larger-than-life gods and epic wars, or it could be told in a way that sees these gods and goddesses as humans. Humans with unmatched power, but humans nonetheless. It's also fascinating because there was never one definitive translation of the myths. Even the loose structure of the timeline can be experimented with in different ways.

Norse mythology was also passed down orally as opposed to written text for, which means that the stories would fade over time. By only salvaging certain characters or certain myths would leave many plot holes in the stories as they were left to others to interpret. That alone causes debates among scholars as they try to untangle the webs and fill in the blanks. We've even had to scratch our heads at the confusion that it leaves. What were the nine worlds? Were these gods the same person? Did this god even exist? We tried our best to iron it out and explain the wrinkles along the way.

The Viking Age

To begin, we have to give a small history lesson, though. Specifically, we will focus on the Icelandic Vikings. The Scandinavian Vikings mostly inhabited the countries of Denmark,

Norway, and Sweden, but what drove them to pillage and plunder until they ultimately settled in Iceland?

Most Scandinavian people lived on islands or peninsulas, so expansion where they were would have been out of the question. The lands they also inhabited had poor terrain and were not very suitable for farming. Population growth was also happening as well, and with the new advances in agriculture at the time, the life expectancy was longer than it had been. More people on these islands and peninsulas meant that there was an increasing amount of bickering between clans.

Once the pillaging began, some men made their living on this dangerous line of work. This would turn it into a way of life for some. For others, it was exile. Viking law would send criminals off on their own, which meant that pillaging might have taken place at the hands of convicted criminals. Another fuel for pillaging would have been greed. The Vikings had the same needs as everyone else, but they were able to obtain the things they needed through violence. This would have made at least a few Vikings pillage because of their own greed. But why Iceland?

There had been two Viking voyagers that drifted onto the land, but it wasn't until Flóki Vildgerdarson had deliberately gone to Iceland for colonization that interest rose. Ice had blocked Flóki's return to Norway, so he had to stay longer than he hoped to. As he left, he would give it the name of Iceland. When he returned to Norway, he would tell everyone of the inhospitable land of ice and snow, but two members of his crew, Herjolf and Thorolof, said that the island was beautiful. While it was his crew members' praise of the land that encouraged settlement, they kept the name "Iceland" given to it by Flóki.

Interest was fueled by attractive and affordable lands available to voyagers because of the warmer climate of Iceland at the time. They also noted that Iceland had a valuable resource to trade in walrus ivory. While they were known for their pillaging, Vikings often gave up the violent life for a peaceful one wherever they settled. However, they would have already gained a bad reputation along the European coasts. This meant that there was a growing resistance to Vikings, which forced them to seek out settlements and begin a peaceful life. Another reason could have been the taxes that the king was placing on the farmers in Norway.

Some lands were taken freely while some bought or were given land from earlier settlers. There was still some land that was taken in the forceful Viking way. There was also one growing factor that made Iceland appealing to the

Scandinavians.

Christian influence was rapidly spreading across Denmark, Sweden, and Norway. However, in Iceland, there was a sort of tug-of-war game between the Christan missionaries (and their Viking followers who had converted on their own) and the pagans. This back and forth would last for well over a century until Christianity took hold of the country in the year 1000. The rest of the Scandinavian countries had already fallen, as Norway's king had converted two years before that. This left lawmaker and pagan, Thorgeir Thorkelsson in a precarious position of trying to keep the peace in Iceland. When a majority of Icelandic people learned of the king's conversion, he knew they would soon convert as well. Conversion would lead to tension, and Thorkelsson was fearful that further bloodshed would find its way to Iceland. He knew that would be the outcome because it had been happening elsewhere.

Probably not his favorite choice, but in order to avoid civil war, Thorkelsson proposed "one law and one religion" which ratified Christianity into law and "banished" paganism.

When the other Scandinavian countries fell into conversion, they cut all ties with Norse paganism. Iceland, contrarily, was willing to embrace where they had come from and their history as a people. The quotes around banished were also because Thorkelsson made a side note for practicing pagans. While the country had to be Christian, the pagans could continue to worship the old gods in secret. It still gives pagans the short stick, but avoiding war with even more mounting tensions happening was for the best. Yes, Iceland was about to have more heated debates over their country's practices. In the 13th century, the country would be in the midst of a violent political battle. Between transforming politics and the new way of Christian life taking over, the fear of losing their heritage took over.

In order to avoid misunderstandings of their cultural identities and belief systems, it became important for Icelandic individuals to find a method of preservation. Stories that were only passed forward by word of mouth, such as children learning when playing the game of "telephone," the end product might compromise cultural integrity. So, for the first time, Icelandic people wrote out Viking lore and Norse mythology to preserve who they were.

Viking lore, also known as "sagas" would be tales of the past, but they were tales about regular men and women. Occasionally, the gods were mentioned, but they were given much more human qualities than the already human versions painted in the Eddas. This was unheard of in this time frame, and it still is a feat for what they accomplished. Those sagas would be the earliest versions of what would become the modern novel. The stories would have a hero, a problem, a story structure, and then they would have a conclusion.

To preserve the Norse mythology, they would have to turn to the "rock stars" of the Viking Age, the Skalds, or more so what the Skalds were known for. Their claim to fame was the art of poetry. To the Vikings, poetry was nothing to scoff at. Poetry was considered to be a gift handed to humans from Odin himself, so the Skalds were basically revered in Norse culture since they were given this gift by the Allfather. They were also the reason Norse mythology would survive because they had kept the myths alive just long enough to make it to written form. That is how we got the second half of the preservation with the Eddas.

The Imperfect Collections

The Eddas had the same effect that the sagas did. They showed just how powerful the oral traditions were, especially in Iceland. The wording, grammar, and syntax were all unique enough that they could be time-stamped to when they were written. This is especially true with *The Poetic Edda.*

There was an issue, as we would discover years after they were put into the world. The problem with the surviving bodies of Norse literature is a lot of components are missing. The Eddas mention many gods and goddesses, but the stories really only involve around 10, and even those that are mentioned are done so sparingly. This makes it hard to think of a god-like Tyr in high regard when he's relegated to a couple of poems. We just had to accept that when *The Poetic Edda* was compiled, there would be a lot that is lost to us. Were those minor gods just forgotten in order to preserve the dominant stories? Unless another Edda were to be uncovered, this will be all that we have to work with.

It's important to remember that those who compiled the Eddas were influenced by Christianity, so some elements of the stories may have been changed to reflect new ideas and understandings of the world. While preserving tradition was important to the compilers, it's difficult to know the extent to which conversion may have affected their work. Some stories can be analyzed through a Christian lens, possibly for this reason, or can be seen to contain some Christian embellishments.

At the beginning of *The Prose Edda*, the gods were the only heroes traveling from Rome to Scandinavia. This *could* have been written in because they were trying to tie their history with the widely accepted values. Basically telling the church that they really liked what they did to the place while snubbing their nose at them. What makes this Edda strange is how it switches over from describing them as mere mortals to talking about the Aesir and Vanir as gods. He would refer to them as the larger-than-life figures that created the world and had fantastic adventures. There may be a reason, but we will get into that in a second.

The Poetic Edda suffered the same fate as there are a few of the verses that just look like a Christian revisionist history. This was the same way that the sagas would treat those who believed in Odin. They were described as uncivilized brutes, an idea that carried over in tellings centuries after...

It's also important to note that all of these compilations come from Iceland. Therefore, there is evidence of Icelandic cultural influence within the text that would not be present otherwise. Mentions of Sweden and the Baltic regions were often referred to as "Mirkwood" where dragons and savage men lived, and Swedish Vikings were often the villains in the sagas.

The primary reason why the Eddas are so important is that they can help us form the foundations of how Norse mythology as we know it took shape.

The Prose Edda

Icelandic poet, politician, and historian Snorri Sturluson would put together the *Prose Edda* somewhere around the year 1220. While this contains many stories about Norse mythology, it's important to remember that this was mostly put together for the sake of protecting the skaldic style and less about preserving the gods.

That was just a bonus. This Edda starts off with Snorri talking about the Aesir and Vanir as if they were normal people. Then the tone shifts back to referring to them as gods, so it is unclear just what Snorri believed. However, perhaps this was the safest way to keep the stories alive. The Christian world would see it as a fantastical story and not as heresy.

Snorri's Edda or the "Younger Edda" were put together because skaldic poetry was delivered in such a unique way. The Edda would be the way future generations could understand the subtle use of alliteration or the many heavy worded metaphors (kennings).

This collection would divide into three books after the prologue: Gylfaginning, Skáldskaparmál, and the Háttatal.

- **Gylfaginning:** This could be seen under different translations as "The Tricking/Beguiling/Deluding of Gylfi." This would serve as the teaching tool for what Icelandic poetry really was without trying to break it down into an actual lesson. The story itself was about King Gylfi's disguised journey into Asgard to interact with the Aesir. The gods then trick Gylfi into believing the lore without believing it themselves. He learns about the gods, creation, destruction, and the rest of Norse mythology in a completely metaphysical sense.

- **Skáldskaparmál:** "The Language of Poetry" would be delivered as a dialogue between Aegir (god of the sea) and Bragi (god of poetry). The origin of kennings was given, followed by kennings for various people, places, and things. This would go to Bragi, explaining the poetic language in greater detail. In particular, it goes over "heiti" or the concept of poetic words that are non-periphrastic ("steed" in place of "horse").

- **Háttatal:** "Tally of Meters" would use mostly Snorri's own poems, but this would be the section of the book that would point out that each poem was written in syllabic meters. This is because the poems relied on the number of syllables in each line. So many of the Norse poems relied on that and relied heavily on drawn-out lines, kennings, and alliteration.

So while the first section provided context to the gods, it wasn't until the next Edda was discovered that more insight into the entirety of Norse mythology was provided.

The Poetic Edda

While Snorri's work was given 50 years prior, the *Poetic Edda* is referred to as the "Elder Edda" because the poetry dates from earlier than the 9th century. This is a collection of around three dozen of the Norse poems. While it is the largest collection of the poems, it still is not all of them. There was no author named, but the intent seems to be the preservation of Viking tradition. The poems offer vivid descriptions of the emotional states of the gods and heroes they were about. These poems would also list the women of the culture as brave warriors.

There are two subject matters in the *Prose Edda*. There were poems of the gods and goddesses and the poems of heroes. The poems of the gods have the stories most told today: creation, Ragnarok, the battle of Aesir and Vanir, and more which are our inspirations for some stories in this book.

The heroic poems feature either human, elf, or dwarf protagonists. These stories showed up in the sagas as well. Can we say "reboot?" While we will get to the portrayal of the gods throughout pop culture as well, it should be noted that Tolkien would go through the poems for inspiration. Many of those would turn into the atmosphere, plot lines, and character names that showed up in *The Hobbit* and *The Lord of the Rings*.

Modern Norse Paganism

While the stories lived on, adoption of a new Christian system of belief removed pagan myths from prominence. However, Christianity would lose its grip. More people have lately sought out the ideas of paganism to adopt and adapt to a modern culture. People who research and come to identify with these beliefs tend to be spiritual and find a more personal meaning beyond religion. Like Odin, they thirst for deeper knowledge. Rune readings have increased in popularity and rival the love that people give to tarot cards. While some embrace the term "heathen," many choose to use Asatru. It should be noted here and now that both Heathen and Asatru groups have had to defend their movement against those trying to promote a racist agenda. Odinism is purely a macho, white supremacist movement that tries to turn the beauty of Norse paganism into something awful.

History of the Asatru

Begun in the Summer of 1972 during the Summer Solstice in Iceland and recognized as a religion the following year, Asatru follows the religion as it was practiced during pre-Christian times. This means that they base their faith in the Eddas and other teachings and follow a polytheistic path. The religion has spread across Iceland, Norway, Sweden, Denmark, and has a small following throughout the United States and England.

The Beliefs of Asatru

The Asatru believe the gods are sort of living beings who are active in what happens in the world. They believe in the Aesir to represent leadership, the Vanir who represent earth and nature, and the Jotnar who symbolize destruction and chaos.

In the afterlife, they believe that those who live dishonorably will be sent to Niflheim. Those who died in battle would go to Valhalla to live among the gods, and the rest would go to Hel where they would have calmness and peace.

The Norse Gods Live

This was important to this story, because this is how we have been able to hold on to the Norse gods 1000 years after they could have been snuffed from existence. They are now no longer just myths, but they have found their way back to guiding people as religious figures.

CHAPTER 2
LET'S START FROM THE BEGINNING

In order to know how the characters themselves, we still need to know how they came into existence. The story of creation in Norse mythology is so astonishing and rich that it should definitely be part of this text as well.

From the Abyss

Before anything existed, there was a vast nothingness known as Ginnungagap. From this expansive void, two realms on opposite ends would come into existence. The first was Niflheim, dark land of ice, frost, and fog. Niflheim would appear on the northern side of the emptiness. On the other, Muspelheim, a land so hot that it was made of fire, lava, and smoke. From Niflheim, the Élivágar, icy rivers flowed down the mountains onto the plains of Ginnungagap. These rivers would solidify into a dense layer that would grow in all directions.

We now have a land of fire and a land of ice, both surrounding this emptiness. The warm air and sparks from Muspelheim would meet with the icy air from Niflheim and begin to melt it. From these drippings of water, the first jötunn (giant) was formed. Also formed was Audhumla, a giant cow whose name fittingly means "abundance of humming." Ymir would feed on Audhumla as she would lick from a salty ice block.

As Ymir slept, the sweat from under his arms made more giants. One of these giants was male and the other was female. His legs would pair together to form his third child, a son named Thrudgelmir. This would be the first family of jötar (ice giants), but Ymir would produce more giants from his sweat every time he slept. These giants were happily feeding on Audhumla as she uncovered something from that ice block. This would end up being a problem for the giants.

One day, she uncovered some hair from the block. The second day would have her uncovering a head. She kept licking the salt block, and she would reveal the rest of the body on the third day. She uncovered the first of the Aesir gods, Buri. Buri would somehow have a son named Borr. Borr would marry Bestla, the daughter of the giant Bolthorn. They then had three half-gods, half-giant children. There was Vili, Ve, and the one who would become the Allfather, Odin.

A Giant Slain, A World Created

The Aesir had a giant problem in the most literal sense. They were bothered because giants were outnumbering the gods. Ymir was going to keep sweating, which meant that there were going to be more giants all the time. There was only one solution to this. Ymir had to die. They couldn't just attack a giant directly, so they waited until Ymir was asleep.

A bloody battle ensued, but the brothers would use all their strength and finish Ymir. The blood from the giant poured out with such force that all but two giants drowned in the flood. The two survivors were Bergelmir and his wife who hopped on a boat and got out of dodge. They would keep the giant race going, though, and would be the parents of ogres, enchanters, warlocks, and witches. One of those witches would give birth to all the wolves that inhabited the world.

With Ymir slaughtered, the brothers would drag the body to the center of Ginnungagap and begin harvesting the giant's remains to create the world. His blood would become the oceans, rivers, and lakes. The giant's flesh was turned into the land, and vegetation was made by his hair. His skull would become the sky and his brains would be the clouds. Ymir's bones would become the mountains while his teeth would be turned into rocks. The brothers then grabbed some sparks from Muspelheim and turned them into the skull that would shine in the dark. We know those sparks as stars now.

As Odin and his brothers walked the beach of this new world they created, they found two trees—one of ash and one of elm. Odin gave them life and spirit, Ve gave them movement and intelligence, and Vili would give them their ultimate form, along with feelings and the five senses we know today. Ask and Embla became the first two humans. The gods would then take Ymir's eyebrows and make a fence around this new world to protect the humans. Thus, Midgard was formed.

Day and Night/Sun and Moon

Note: There are contradictions about how night and day came to be. One of those versions is that they are gods, the other is human based. So, we will tell them both.

First, let's say there are no humans, and so we would have to believe in Dagr and Nótt (Day and Night). Nótt was the goddess of night and the grandmother to Thor. She was also the mother of Dagr. Odin would give both the mother and son a horse and chariot to ride across the heavens until Ragnarök arrived. Nótt would be pulled by Hrímfaxi (frost mane) and the foam from the horse's mouth would make the morning dew. Dagr would ride behind Skinfaxi (shining mane) and bring about the daylight.

The other story of this was set after Midgard was established and populated by humans. One such human, Mundilfari, would have a son and a daughter. He felt his children were so beautiful and were so luminous that he would name his son Mani and his daughter Sol (moon and sun, respectively). The gods took offense to human children being held in such high regard. They dealt with Mundailfari's arrogance by taking his children and putting them up in the sky. They weren't being overly cruel, though, as they gave each child a chariot.

Sol's chariot would be pulled by Árvakr and Alsvidr ("early rising" and "very quick"). The horses were fitted with bellows by the gods to cool them down as they rode, and her chariot would have Svalin, a shield that would protect everything below the flames. Mani's chariot would only be pulled by one horse, so he felt he could make up for this by stealing two Midgard children (Bil and Yuki) to help him drive his chariot. Not everything in mythology follows a moral code.

In both stories, though, they were each pursued by a wolf that would be the son of Odin's slayer, Fenrir. Sköll (Treachery) would pursue Sol/Dagr. Once Sköll would catch up, he would devour the daylight. This would only happen during Ragnarok, though. However, it was the reasoning for why daytime would feel as if it would pass so quickly because Sol was in fear of being caught.

Mani or Nótt's wolf was Hati (Hate). Unfortunately for Mani, he was not as quick as Sol. Therefore, Hati would manage to get a bite of him until he would make his escape to heal. This would explain the phases of the moon. No science, just wolves.

The Dwarves and The Elves

As the gods were creating this new world, they noticed worms crawling up from the soil that had been made from the flesh of Ymir. These worms were pitch black in color, and so the gods would make them into dwarves, or dökkálfar (dark elves). They made a home for them underground in their own world of Nidavellir/Svartalfheim.

They also noticed a more beautiful creature emerging and would turn them into the ljósálfar (light elves). The light elves would be sent to Alfheim. The elves would be the most intertwined with humans as elves could cause and cure illnesses. Humans and elves can also interbreed and produce half-elf, half-human children who appear as human but have magical abilities.

Odin and his brothers were becoming fearful that the sky they created would suddenly collapse. So, they sent four of the newly created dwarves in opposite directions to hold the sky up. These dwarves would be Nordi, Sundri, Austri, and Vestri—or better known as North, South, East, and West. The other dwarves would inhabit Svartalfheim and become masterful craft workers for the gods.

After they had given homes to humans, dwarves, elves, and giants, the gods needed a place to call home as well, so from the plains of Idavoll, they made the Bifrost (the rainbow bridge) and crossed to their new world of Asgard. The remaining giants would take over their own world of Jotunheim.

Yggdrasil and the Nine Worlds

We have eight worlds so far. Hel makes nine, but there was no real clarity on how it came to be except that it could have been located in the roots of Yggdrasil, which we will talk about now.

Yggdrasil

Its branches lie in the heavens and its roots in the underworld. This sacred tree in Norse mythology stretches into other religions and mythologies around the world. The trunk of this tree is the center of the Norse cosmos, and the nine worlds are spread delicately along—held by the branches and roots of the tree. All life from gods and giants to the humans and the dead depends on the well-being of Yggdrasil. Its shiver signals the arrival of Ragnarok.

The tree is tended to by Urd, Verdandi, and Skuld—the three Norns that roughly represent past, present, and future. They tend to the tree by watering it from the Well of Urd (Well of Fate) because as the Eddas would show; the tree was not only sacred to Norse beliefs, but it was also still a normal tree, which means the tree could die. If the tree dies, *all* things will cease to exist.

Because it is still a tree, it is alive and hosts several animals. The malicious dragon, Nidhogg, and several snakes dwell at the bottom and feed at its roots. An eagle sits at the very top, holding a type of vigil over the cosmos. Ratatoskr (Drill Tooth), the squirrel runs between the roots and the branches, delivering messages or insults on behalf of the eagle and the dragon. Feeding on Yggdrasil's leaves is four stags—Dainn, Dvalinn, Duneyrr, and Durathror.

Yggdrasil has three major roots: the first lies in Midgard, another lies in Jotunheim, and the last lies in Helheim. While *Poetic Edda* only lists the Well of Urd, *Prose Edda* says that there are three wells for each of the roots. The Well of Urd was actually in the sky and was the place the gods held a daily council. This is likely the Midgard well given its proximity to Asgard. Hvergelmir (Bubbling Cauldron or Roaring Kettle) was under the root that lay in Hel and would stretch to Niflheim. This also makes sense, given that both Hel and Niflheim are described at different times as lands for the dead. Mimir's well would lie in Jotunheim, which we will see more of later.

The Nine Worlds

The nine worlds are depicted differently depending on the text of origin. Some books split Nidavellir and Svartalfheim into separate entities, which leaves Helheim off the tree. We could even speculate that it was Svartalfheim that combined with Alfheim instead since both of their inhabitants were elves. This could be formidable given that one famous Marvel movie put dwarves and dark elves into separate worlds. That will be for a later chapter, but let's look at the nine as they are best represented.

Midgard: This is what we know as Earth today, and it roughly means "Middle Enclosure." Midgard is directly below Asgard and above Helheim, and it is also surrounded by an impassable ocean that is surrounded by a giant serpent, Jormungandr, that circles the entire world.

Asgard: Home of the gods that sits above Midgard. Inside the gates of Asgard is Valhalla where those who die bravely in battle on Midgard will go after being chosen by the Valkyries that hover over the battlegrounds.

One noticeable thing is the -gard suffix in both

Midgard and Asgard. This is distinct because of the ancient Germanic idea of innangard and utangard. Innangard (inside the fence) would be the peaceful and orderly way of life, and anything utangard (outside the fence) would be chaotic. So while you were in Midgard or Asgard, there would be a sense of stability. However, if you were to step out of those worlds, things would become more chaotic.

Vanaheim: There were two types of gods and goddesses in Norse mythology. There was the Aesir living on Asgard, but Vanaheim would be home to the Vanir gods and goddesses. Given the accounts of who the Vanir were, this is mostly tied to "nature," "magic," and "spirituality" as we know it today. The best clue of where this world sat on Yggdrasil was from the poem "Lokasenna" ("The Taunting of Loki"). In the poem, it described Njord traveling east to Asgard. This would be fitting, since they were gods and goddesses, after all.

Jotunheim: This would be the land of the giants. Jotunheim would comprise rocks, wilderness, and dense forests. Besides that, there was no fertile land. The giants could only live on the fish from the rivers and the animals from the forests. Even though the Aesir and the giants were always in a battle—Odin, Thor, and others had loves that were giants. Jotunheim would also be the homeland of Loki until he was taken in by the Aesir. The giants had a version of Asgard known as Utgard.

Alfheim: Another land on the opposite side of Asgard. This would be the home of the light elves. Ruled by Freyr, these elves are considered guardian angels. Because they are not quite Aesir or Vanir, these are the minor gods of nature and fertility. They have the ability to aid or hinder humans with their magic and can inspire poets.

Niflheim: Because Niflheim only really exists through the works of Snorri, it's hard to gauge if Niflheim existed. This would be the primordial land of ice, and without it, there would be more holes in the plot of creation. In Snorri's works, he would interchange the word "Niflhel." This could also be taken as more of embellishment of Hel. It could also be thought of as a sub-level of Hel, like Judecca was in Dante's inferno. This would be the place in Hell for the worst of the worst to be trapped in an icy eternity. This makes sense, given that Hvergelmir was the well that stretched from the root in Hel into Niflheim.

Muspelheim: This is the primordial land of fire that assisted in the world's creation. Again, this is from the works of Snorri. However, without it, there is no straightforward story of creation. It is also important to Ragnarok, as this was the home of Surtr, who was a sworn enemy of the Aesir. In the other poetic works, Surtr would come from the south with a flaming sword to snuff out the world ("end of the world through fire") and set Asgard ablaze.

Nidavellir/Svartalfheim: We already went over the theory that Svartalfheim was part of Alfheim in a sort of light side/dark side of the moon. However, because there was no real distinction between the dark elves and the dwarves, they were used interchangeably just as the name of their world was.

Hel: Ruled by the goddess of the same name, only the *Prose Edda* describes this as an unpleasant place. Hel could have ruled over both Hel and Niflheim. In other works, Hel was simply a place for the dead that did not die honorably in a battle to go to Valhalla or died as dishonorable people to be sent to the icy land of

Niflheim. Hel would be the place where the souls would just spend an afterlife doing the same things they did while in Midgard. No glory, no torment, just a place in the afterlife akin to purgatory.

CHAPTER 3
FREYA

Who Was Freya?

Freya (the lady) was the Vanir goddess of blessings, love, and fertility. She not only lusted for other figures in Norse mythology, but they would lust for her in return. She was the type of goddess who could be gentle or fierce depending on the moment.

Being Vanir meant that Freya was a practitioner of magic, in particular sedir. Sedir was potent magic that allowed the practitioner to see the coming fates and work within it to change the outcomes. This was very powerful and was viewed as witchcraft by the gods, even though they desired the magic Freya had introduced to them.

Despite her displays of power, Freya was known as one of the more gentle of the gods. Thor was violent and was more of a "vanquish first, ask questions later" kind of god. Odin and Loki were tricksters and would rely on their cunning before their brute strength. Freya would accomplish her goals by using gifts, her beauty, and her pleasure. She was seen as unselfish, but Freya also had a darker side. She enjoyed the blood of battle. In fact, she would get first pick and half of the warriors killed in battle. Half would go to Valhalla, and the other half would go to Freya's realm, called Fólkvangr.

Freya had several other names (Freja, Freyia, Freyja, Fröja, Frøya, Frøjya, Frua, and others), which might have meant that Freya was actually Odin's wife, Frigg. This is either the same person with distinct personalities or another version of the same goddess. Thanks to translations, we are left with a giant blank, so we will try our best to think of them as separate entities.

Freya was the archetype for what would be the seeress in Norse mythology, as she was a leading practitioner of sedir. She would only be rivaled by Odin in this respect. After being sent to live in Asgard, Freya made her home in the Fólkvangr (field of the host) palace of Sessrúmnir (seat room).

Because she was more peaceful than bloodthirsty, Freya didn't have any signature war weapons. Instead, she adorned unique pieces in her war attire. One of these was a cloak of falcon feathers that could give its wearer the gift of flight, or it could disguise anyone who was doing favors for Freya. Her prized possession was a necklace known as Brísingamen (gleaming torc). This necklace to her was what Mjölnir was to Thor. She went to the dwarves to get her own special gift, and they would do it for a steep price. Freya then had to spend a night with each of the dwarves, so once she had this necklace, she guarded it with her life. Freya also had a glistening chariot that was pulled by two cats, and she had an animal familiar named Hildisvíni (battle swine).

Freya was the daughter of Njordr, the Vanir god of sea, sailing, fishing, wealth, and the fertility of crops. Her mother is speculated to be Nerthus, but that is only speculation. Freya also had one brother, Freyr. Along with Njordr and Freyr, these were the Vanir gods that were given to Asgard after the Aesir-Vanir War.

In her later years, she married Odr, a mysterious god who would leave on long journeys. His frequent absence would cause the goddess to cry golden tears. She had two daughters with Odr, Hnoss, and Gersemi.

This is sometimes used as evidence that Freya was Frigg as well. Odr was gone on long journeys, and Odin was infamous for leaving home for long periods at a time.

The Aesir-Vanir War

Before her life in Asgard, Freya would travel around town to town practicing sedir. While it was a very powerful form of magic, everyone would employ her services to get their fates changed. She would take on the name Heidr (Bright) as she entered Asgard. The gods were immediately taken to the goddess and paid for her service. Beautiful and magical? There was a lot for the gods of Asgard to love and want. This would go on for some time until the gods ran into a "moral" problem. The problem was, eventually, the gods realized that they were using her magic for their own selfish reasons. Instead of blaming themselves, though, they would blame Freya for even bringing that witchcraft into Asgard because they couldn't face their own shortcomings. They're gods and couldn't take the blame, so they dubbed her "Gullveig" (gold greed).

They did just as we would expect of people terrified of a witch. They took the beautiful goddess, stabbed her repeatedly with their spears, and burned her alive. To the gods' surprise, Freya would only emerge from the ashes. They set fire to her again, but Freya would return for the second time. Once again, they burned her, and for the third time, she would rise. The gods then imprisoned her while they tried to decide what to do with this "witch."

Word would eventually get back to the Vanir of how their goddess was treated. They became angry at the Aesir, and this led to bitterness and distrust between both groups of gods. The Vanir weren't about to stand for the punishment they gave to Freya, so they prepared for war. However, Odin would know what the Vanir were planning, so the Aesir prepared themselves for battle.

In the beginning battles, the Vanir would gain the upper hand by using their powers of magic to tear the walls of Asgard down. The Aesir would make the same efforts in Vanaheim by using their brute strength. This would begin a vicious back and forth between the gods. Both sides used their different methods, but both would see the same results, which was absolutely no gain.

This would go on for what seemed like an eternity, but both the Aesir and Vanir eventually grew weary of being in constant stalemate and would call for a truce. The custom between them would be established that they were to trade hostages. Therefore, the Vanir sent Freya, Freyr, and their father Njord east to Asgard. The Aesir would send Hoenir and Mimir west to Vanaheim.

As we learned from her biography, Freya did not fare too badly living in Asgard. Not much is known about Njordr after the war, but he probably lived a good life among the Aesir. Freyr would eventually rule over Alfheim, so the Vanir hostages made out exceptionally well.

However, the same could not be said about the Aesir that would live in Vanaheim. Vanir gods would turn to Hoenir for advice, seeing that he was a very handsome god, but while Hoenir was handsome, he was not all that intelligent. He couldn't deliver solid advice without Mimir by his side. Many times, Hoenir would be alone during Vanir council, and many times he would give them the same answer: "Let the others decide."

The Vanir gods got annoyed and then irate because they felt as if the Aesir gave them a terrible deal. They then did what any rational god would have done. The Vanir seized Mimir, threw him to the ground, and beheaded him. They then sent the head back to Asgard in a "Tell Odin it was us" fashion.

Odin was upset about the loss of Mimir. He cradled the head and recited magic chants over it. He then covered it and embalmed it with herbs to preserve it. This allowed Odin to gain even more knowledge from Mimir.

Odin could have lost his own head in anger, but both sides were still not ready to reignite a battle that would be evenly matched. There would have been no end, only destruction. So instead of Aesir-Vanir War II they would then come together around a cauldron to make peace. Both Aesir and Vanir gods spit into the cauldron, and from that saliva, the creature Kvasir would be created. Kvasir was the wisest of all beings and would become the sign of harmony between the two groups of gods.

While this was a significant battle in Norse mythology, it was the only time that the two tribes would experience any tension. After the war, there would be a peaceful time for the gods.

CHAPTER 4
ODIN

Who Was Odin?

The Allfather Odin is still the most worshiped figure in Norse paganism from the Middle Ages, even in the resurgence of popularity of Norse mythology. Odin was a god of ecstasy and inspiration, held the highest regard for all the gods and goddesses.

Even though he was thought of as a brutish military mind who craved a good fight, he would go against expectation. He would be a successful warrior, and it was claimed that he could never lose a battle. He was also known as a highly intellectual man, and that was his most prominent role in the myths. As opposed to sitting on his throne in Valhalla where he could see across the cosmos, he would travel all the nine realms in disguise as a traveler. This was because while Odin was relentless in battle, he was also relentless in his search for knowledge.

Gaining wisdom about anything and everything was his ultimate passion. Odin wanted wisdom about his enemies, his future, and everything that would happen in the worlds he created. He sought out shamans, seers, necromancers, the dead, and anyone who would give him what he wanted. Odin also had a unique way of speaking as he would do in poems and riddles, which may be a sign of his preference for wit over brutality. Like his half-brother Loki, Odin could shape-shift, allowing him access to all places throughout the nine realms.

Odin's name roughly translated to "the Fury." Other translations would be "the furious," "the passionate," "the inspired," or "the inspiring." Any of these names would fit someone who was so passionate about knowledge that he would go through any means to get it. Given that he had such a vast knowledge of all things, Odin would bring that fury and passion into his well thought out plans. This also meant that no matter what form he was taking, he would channel all of his focus into it. This made Odin an inspiring figure for everyone under him.

The primary things Odin would be known for was his wit and wisdom. He learned the art of sedir and would be just as skilled in the magic as the Vanir goddess who brought it to the Aesir. With that poetic way of speaking, he often got the humans on Midgard to do uncharacteristic things. While he was the highest of the gods, he had his own fun being a trickster like Loki.

Odin would carry a staff or a spear (depending on if he was a god or traveler). He would often take Mimir's head with him in order to gain further insight, advice, and secrets. When he would decide to be home in Asgard, he would sit on his throne, Hlidskjalf, that lay in Valhalla. This allowed him to overlook all the nine realms. Odin had animal familiars as well. Geri and Freki were two wolves that would travel with Odin and search for the bodies of slain warriors. Again, the constant seeker of knowledge, Odin also had two ravens called Huninn and Muninn (Thought and Memory). They would leave Odin at dawn, spying on all the worlds, returning each night to deliver their news to their master.

We would see from creation that Odin was the son of Bestla, the frost giant, and Borr. The creature licked out of a block of salt ice. He had his brothers, Vili and Vé, but they would not appear again after creation, though their sons would appear after Ragnarök.

Odin would marry Frigg, and they would be the parents to Baldur. Odin had lovers and children, most likely throughout his travels. He would have Thor with the giant Jord. With Gridr, another giant, he would father Vidarr, whose future role would revive Odin during Ragnarök. With yet another giant, Rindr, he would father Valí. Valí's only purpose was to avenge the slain Baldur.

Odin was also the half-brother of Loki, the giant who would be accepted by the Aesir. While the sources aren't great, Odin is also most likely the father of Tyr, Heimdall, Bragi, and Hodr. Maybe calling him the "Allfather" is a little too on the nose.

Odin's Quests

While Odin was considered the wisest of the gods, he was still not as knowledgeable as Mimir. Odin knew Mimir would gain his knowledge by drinking from Mimisbrunnr (Mimir's Well). This meant that Odin would have to travel to Jotunheim to drink from the same well.

When he arrived at the well, he spoke to Mimir's head (he was preserved and enchanted). He wanted to drink from the well and gain the wisdom that Mimir had. Mimir would tell Odin that the price to drink from the well was steep. In exchange for that drink, Odin would have to give up an eye.

Not the one to back down from gaining knowledge, Odin would gouge out his own eye and throw it into the well. He then filled a horn full of the well's water and downed it. It's unclear what knowledge Odin was seeking from the well, but once he drank it, he would be unmatched in intellect by any god in all the realms.

On another quest, Odin would set out to gain knowledge of the runes to deliver to the humans in Midgard. The runes would use symbols that worked as letters, each with their own sound and meaning. These would embody cosmic powers. We can see rune readings even today, a long time away from when Odin would make one of his biggest sacrifices.

To understand the runes, Odin hung himself on the cosmic tree at the center of the universe, Yggdrasil. Hanging from this tree over the well of Urd, he would stab himself with his spear and fast for nine days. The runes then spoke to Odin, revealing their true meanings and full understanding. After Odin learned to decipher them, he then spread his own knowledge with everyone. A selfless act from the major sacrifice Odin made.

In a poem, Odin mentions three maidens. By what we know about Yggdrasil, Odin most likely got the runes from the Norns who tend to the cosmic tree.

The Mead of Poetry

This would be a spiritual successor to the Aesir-Vanir War. The gods had created Kvasir, the smartest creature in all the realms. He would travel, giving everyone he encountered the answers they sought. He enjoyed his newfound fame as he traveled far and wide. Unfortunately, Kvasir was about to meet his demise.

Two dwarves, Fjalar and Galar, invited Kvasir to

their home. As soon as he arrived, he was murdered by the dwarves, and they would brew a batch of mead with the creature's blood. When the gods questioned them, the dwarves would only say that Kvasir choked on his own wisdom.

The dwarves were on a killing spree. Shortly after the death of Kvasir, they took the giant Gilling and drowned him in the sea just for their own amusement. After learning her husband was dead, Gilling's wife cried. The sound of her crying would irritate Fjalar and Galar, so they dropped a stone on her head, killing her instantly.

This would be the last of their fun because Gilling's son, Suttung, learned of his father's murder. He captured the dwarves and took them to an area with low tides. He then laid them on a reef that would soon be underwater. The dwarves, obviously terrified of their impending doom, pleaded with Suttung to let them go. Suttung would give them what they wanted in exchange for the special mead the dwarves made. The dwarves naturally chose self-preservation and gave Suttung the mead. The giant would then hide the mead in a chamber beneath the mountain Hnitbjorg, and place his daughter Gunnlod to watch over his fresh supply.

So, what does any of this have to do with Odin? Remember, this is a god who is in an endless pursuit of knowledge. He was not about to have a special mead trapped in a giant's cave. It was not a selfish endeavor, since Odin wanted to share the mead with those he deemed worthy.

Odin then disguised himself as a farmhand and went to the farm of Suttung's brother, Baugi. He found nine other farmhands mowing hay for Baugi. He approached them and offered to sharpen their scythes. The workers would wonder at how much more productive they were with sharper axes. They would ask the traveler if he would sell them this amazing sharpening stone. Odin agreed on the stipulation they would pay a high price. He then took the stone and threw it in the air, and none of the farmhands thought to put their scythes down. They would end up killing each other in the rush for the stone.

The trickster Odin would then go to Baugi's door and introduce himself as Bölverkr (Worker of Misfortune). He would tell Baugi that his nine servants had needlessly killed each other earlier and offered to do their work instead for a sip of mead. Baugi was not in charge of the mead but, seeing as he needed the work done, he would agree to this farmhand's deal.

The growing season was over and Odin had

delivered on his promise. Baugi then had to take a disguised Odin to Suttung for his sip of mead. However, Suttung would not hear of it and refused a meager farmhand with a sip of *his* mead. Baugi thought he had gotten out of the deal, but Bölverkr reminded him that a deal was a deal and Baugi had to give him a sip. They would then go to Gunnlod's dwelling and find a chamber that Baugi knew was close to the mead. Odin then handed the giant an auger to drill through the cave walls. The giant finished once, but when Odin tested it by blowing into it, he was greeted with a face full of dust and rock. He would then demand that Baugi finish drilling the hole out, so the giant once again complied. This second attempt was a success, so Odin transformed into a snake to fit through the hole to the other side. In a desperate moment, Baugi tried to stab him with the auger, but Odin made it through intact.

He then needed to get past Suttung's daughter,

so Odin shapeshifted again. This time, he would take the form of a very charming man. He then made a deal that, if he spent three nights with her, she would give him three sips of mead. Gunnlod agreed, and on the third night, Odin was given access to the chamber where the mead was kept. There, he found three vats of Kvasir's brew, and he drank all of them.

Making his escape from the cave, Odin turned into an eagle and bolted back to Asgard to deliver the mead. Suttung learned of what happened and, as an eagle, gave chase to Odin. Seeing that their chief was being pursued by a giant, the gods would set out containers for Odin to deposit the mead. Odin beat out the giant, and Suttung would have to go back home with none of his ill-gotten mead.

Odin then had to regurgitate the mead into the new vats. He was still an eagle at this time, and when he filled the vats, a few drops fell onto Midgard. These drops of the mead gave all the bad/mediocre poets and scholars their lackluster abilities. The best poets, however, got to get this Odin-aged Kvasir mead by the Allfather himself. Unless any of us have been sought by the head of all gods and been hand delivered mead, then I would assume we are all mediocre poets.

CHAPTER 5
LOKI

Who Was Loki?

While Odin was a trickster, Loki was *the* trickster. He was known as a shapeshifter and for the many deceptions that he would play across the nine realms. Loki was never shown to have a motive for what he did. Some of his tricks would get the other gods in predicaments, but sometimes he would use his deceitfulness to get the gods out of trouble as well.

Loki was a part of the Aesir and was seen as one of the four rulers of the gods. While Odin, Thor, and Freya had clear goals for keeping order, Loki would often end up having his allegiance questioned. What makes Loki's place in Asgard unique is that it had always been fated that he would side with the giants during Ragnarök.

In short, Loki was neither good nor evil. He was simply Loki, and his greatest love was mischief itself. While the other gods would represent things that were good and pure, Loki would represent that the space between good and evil was less clear than people would like to believe.

Loki's name in Old Norse was closely related to "logi," which means fire. This is fitting because Loki was unpredictable and likely to get out of control. Also, if you play with fire too much, of getting burned. In other Germanic translations, his name could be traced to "knot" or "tangle."

He would tangle the gods in whatever mess he got into, and much like having a knot in your back, he was sometimes just unpleasant to be around.

While he was a god, Loki rarely partook in actual battle and never carried a weapon. He relied solely on his cunningness and the ability to shape-shift. Contrary to modern portrayal, Loki had no unique clothing or helmets. Any items he used were usually on loan from the other gods, such as Freya's cloak.

Loki was born to the giant Fárbauti and minor goddess Laufey (sometimes known as Nál). He had two brothers, Helblindi and Byleistr, who were giants as well. By some accounts, Loki and Odin were half-brothers as well. Loki married eventually to the giant Sigyn. It isn't much about her except that she was the mother of their sons, Váli and Narvi. Like many gods, Loki had a lover outside of his marriage. He and Angrboda would produce the more key offspring: Hel, Jormungandr, and Fenrir. Hel would take over a realm of the same name. Jörmungandr would be Thor's bitter enemy and the sea serpent that would surround Midgard. Fenrir would be the wolf that would be the end of Odin. There were also two other sons who were seldom mentioned.

Loki did have a child of his own as well, in the literal sense. During one of his ventures, he took the form of a mare. This would attract the stallion Svadilfari, and from that, Loki would birth the eight-legged horse Sleipnir. Sleipnir would go on to be Odin's favorite to ride on his travels.

Loki Comes with Gifts

One thing in the versions we see today that is true in the myths is the interesting relationship between the trickster god and Thor. They would ride together on adventures frequently to Jotunheim to do battle or for just their own pleasure. This meant that Thor was often the recipient of Loki's pranks. That's what brings us to the Dwarven Wager.

Thor would marry Sif, the goddess of the fertile Earth. Sif was extremely beautiful and virtuous. Her hair, in particular, held a specific beauty because it was described as golden as the wheat fields. This made gods and giants alike jealous of Thor. One person, in particular, was not exactly jealous, but he saw an opening to cause more chaos.

One night, as the goddess slept, Loki snuck up behind Sif and began to cut all of her hair off. Thor, of course, would hear about this afterward and would not be happy about what Loki had done. Thor would catch the trickster and threaten unspeakable things—broken bones, fed to wolves, and anything an angry Thor could think of. Loki was undoubtedly terrified of what Thor was actually going to do to him, so he swore to fix everything and bargain with the dwarves to get Sif genuine golden hair.

Probably with some vulgarities and more threats, Thor would agree and send Loki on his way. Loki did have a decent heart because he truly wanted to set things right. He arrived at Svartalfheim and met two dwarves, Brokk and Eitri. All dwarves were wonderful craftsmen, but these sons of Ívaldi were renowned for their skills. Loki would then ask if they could make golden hair that would be worthy of the goddess.

The brothers got to work and soon had more than what Loki had come for. These dwarves probably sensed the desperation, and Brokk gave Loki three gifts. The first was hair made of gold for Sif. Except this hair would feel and grow just as natural hair.

The second gift was a ship for Freyr named Skidbladnir. Naturally, this was not just an ordinary ship. It was so long and wide that it could fit every Aesir god on it. Not only could it sail the sea, but it could fly as well. The elves would construct the ship out of the thinnest planks, so when Freyr wasn't using it, she could fold it up and store it in a pouch.

The third gift was Gungir, which was a spear for Odin. Again, the dwarves were the best craftsmen, and this would be no ordinary spear. The spear would have runes carved into its point, likely making it more deadly and precise. This was not only the spear that Odin would stab himself with when trying to gain rune knowledge, but he would throw the spear over Vanaheim at the beginning of the Aesir-Vanir war.

Loki had already gotten more than he originally came for, but his greed would get the better of him again. He would flatter Brokk and make the snide comment to Eitri that he could never make gifts like those. Brokk was a little smarter than that. He made the wager and said if Eitri could deliver the same quality of gifts, he would cut off Loki's head. Loki accepted under the stipulation that they could take his head, but they could not cut at his neck. These dwarves were masters of their craft, and they knew that their bet was a sure thing. Loki would soon lose his head.

The dwarves started to work with Brokk now working the bellows while Eitri crafted. They knew that the metal had to be at the perfect temperature to do craft from metal. Loki knew this as well, and he knew that he appeared on the losing side of the wager. As the dwarves focused on their work, a fly would proceed to bite Brokk on the hand. He was irritated, but he continued to work the bellows. From this, Eitri soon had crafted a golden boar, Gullinbursti.

Loki was a third of the way to being the next Mimir as the dwarves set down new gold for Eitri's second gift. Brokk worked the bellows and was bitten on the neck by the same fly. This caused Brokk further pain, but he endured. Eitri could produce a magnificent golden ring, Draupnir. Loki was now desperate with the dwarves, only needing to produce one more gift.

This last gift was going to be special, and Eitri knew it would be for a courageous god of war. He worked with iron for this next gift and set back to work. Loki knew that if the dwarves were successful, they would come for his head. The twice-bitten Brokk again worked the bellows for his brother, but he was soon bitten again by the fly. This time it was right on his eyelid. Not only was Brokk in pain, he now had blood trickling into his eye. Eitri completed the gift that was now Mjölnir.

Having succeeded in their task, Brokk ventured to Asgard with all six gifts. He was not as confident now, but he hoped the gods would love their gifts and he would get to behead the trickster god. Brokk would present the gods with their gifts while Loki kept a watchful eye over the proceedings.

Brokk presented the Allfather with his gift first. Odin was pleased with a spear that would always kill and never miss. He then fit the new hair on Sif's head, and she was also pleased with her gift. She twirled as the new hair bonded to her as her own. Next was Freyr's new ship, and the Vanir god was excited to have a ship that always had favorable conditions to sail and could be easily stored when not in use! Brokk was now about to deliver Eitri's gifts.

First was the Draupnir, which would go to Odin. While it was magnificent, it was also enchanted. Every ninth night, the ring would produce eight identical rings. Odin could then distribute those to the gods or anyone he deemed worthy. Freyr would get Gullinbursti, the golden boar. Gillunbursti was given the ability to run across the sky and on the earth as fast as a horse, and his golden hair would also light up the darkest areas. Again, Freyr was delighted because his travels would always be prosperous.

Finally, the moment of truth was about to happen. Brokk presented Thor with Mjölnir, the mighty hammer that would smash giants, aid Thor on his quests, and be the greatest thing Captain America could ever hold. Even though they all looked at their gifts in astonishment, they were envious of Thor's hammer. They were envious but named Eitri's gift the greatest of the six. Loki had lost the bet, but he would try to muster one last point for the gods. Mjölnir was amazing, yes, but the handle was far too small. Brokk had been distracted after being bitten by his eye, and it caused the one cosmetic flaw on the hammer.

Brokk then realized that Loki had been the fly the entire time in order to cheat his way to victory. To Loki's dismay, not even the short handle had taken the luster away from the hammer. He was now going to pay his debt and give the dwarf what he wagered. Loki tried to run, but he was stopped by Thor, who held him in place. It was then that he would remind Brokk that he could have the head but not the neck, as per the agreement they had.

There was no way to accomplish a proper beheading without touching the neck, and Brokk would realize the error of the wager. The dwarf was furious at being outsmarted by Loki once again; however, he would still get his payment. Brokk took his knife and some string and sewed Loki's mouth shut, making sure the god could never trick someone again. The gods would all laugh at Loki's expense, and he was humiliated. Loki swore he would get his revenge on the gods one day.

Loki's Flyting

Sometime after the tragic death of Baldur, when the gods had finally moved past the mourning period, they would gather on the island of Hlesey for a feast. This would be Aegir's hall where they would gather, and since Thor and Tyr had brought Hymir's cauldron, he would brew them his finest ale. Thor had taken his leave to Jotunheim, but everyone else filled the hall. Odin and Frigg led the way followed by Sif, the one-armed god Tyr, Njord and his wife Skadi, Freyr and Freya, Odin's son Vidar, and Loki.

This was not all, as the hall was also filled with other gods and many elves. The guests sat down and Aegir's servants, Fimafeng and Eldir, served them. The ale that Aegir had brewed would find its own way into the glasses of the guests. Soon, the emptiness in the hall filled with happy tidings and high praise for the two servants. Loki sat among them, possibly already drunk and his temper flaring with every good word said to the two servants. It became too much for Loki to bear, and he leaped up and killed Fimafeng.

The gods all stood up at once and yelled at Loki. The same god that had aided in the death of the beloved Baldur had just spilled the servant's blood in front of them. They called him mad and chased Loki out of the hall. Once he was gone, the gods had gone back in and the party would resume. Poor Fimafeng never got a proper goodbye.

While he had cowered away in the woods, Loki would return to Aegir's hall. He would then ambush Eldir, the surviving servant, and ask him what the gods had been discussing after his dismissal. Eldir told him they were discussing their feats in battle and comparing their weapons. The servant then followed quickly in telling Loki that the trickster god's name had not been mentioned. Not even once. Edir was told by Loki that he would make his way back inside to fill the gods' hearts with hatred and grief. Loki had a plan, and when Eldir told him they would throw it right back at him, Loki simply warned the servant that whatever he would say, Loki would double the harshness of his reply. This would be the same treatment the gods would receive. Loki then knocked the servant out of the way and made his presence known to the gods and goddesses.

He announced his second arrival to Aegir's hall and would tell them he was thirsty. He wanted more ale, and there were no legal limits in the land of gods. Loki was met with silence, which made his devious heart gleeful. He demanded a place at their table or they would have to tell him he was unwanted and make him leave. The skald Bragi would try to tell Loki that he was, in fact, not welcome to their feast. Loki ignored the poet and addressed Odin instead.

He reminded Odin that they had once made a pact in the form of a blood oath, and Odin had sworn that day he would only drink if Loki was offered one as well. While the chief god was annoyed by his half-brother's presence and his painful reminder, he was still a man of his word.

He told Vidar to move up and to make room for Fenrir's father. He did not wish to have any more trouble or bloodshed that night. Vidar did as he was told, and he poured a fresh cup of ale for Loki. Loki sipped from his cup, and then he began his verbal assault on the gods.

He greeted all the gods and goddesses again, but he would make it a point to say that Bragi was not included in his good wishes. Bragi would try to say that if Loki would just keep quiet that he would give him a horse, a sword, and a ring. Loki would respond by calling Bragi nothing more than a beggar and a coward who never helped the gods in battle. Bragi would tell him that if they were not in Aegir's hall, he would tear his head from his body. Loki could only laugh and reply that Bragi was more woman than god and that heroes didn't talk about their plans.

Idun would speak up, but not to Loki. She told

her husband to not waste words and trade insults during what was supposed to be a jovial occasion. Loki then hurled insults at her, saying she fell in love with her brother's killer (there was no mention of Idun's brother or any such story except in this myth). Idun ignored Loki's abuse and refused to trade insults with him. She also reminded the gods that Bragi (and possibly Loki) was drunk and that she already told her husband to keep his cool.

Gefion would interject and question why anyone would engage with Loki when he obviously hated everyone inside the hall. Loki would try to accuse the goddess of not being as pure as she claimed and had been in bed with someone for a shiny necklace. This is where Loki completely lost his tact and began making up insults to further fan the flames of hatred.

Odin would draw the line at this point because

all the gods and goddesses knew Gefion was the purest of them all and would remain that way. He told Loki that he lost his mind by coming into Aegir's hall and engaging in this verbal tirade. Loki shut him down and told him he would often let his opponents win battles even if they had proven that they were weaker. Odin did not deny that he often showed mercy. Instead, he tried to insult Loki by reminding him about the eight winters the trickster god had lived under the earth, assumed the shape of a woman, and had many children. He would tell Loki that he was a woman through and through. Loki was one step ahead and reminded Odin of a time that he would practice witchcraft (which was a very feminine practice in Norse mythology). Not only did he practice as a witch, but he would move through men while shape-shifted as a witch. Loki would finish him by calling him a woman through and through.

Frigg, wanting to restore order in the hall, told

both Odin and Loki to stop acting like children and keep their insults to themselves. What good would bringing up the past do for either of them? Loki turned his attention to the beautiful goddess. Loki accused Frigg of adultery by sharing a bed with Odin's brothers, Vili and Ve. Frigg responded that if she had Baldur by her side, Loki would surely pay for what he said to her. This would cause the tensions to escalate further when Loki reminded her it was his trickery that ensured she'd never had her son by her side ever again.

Freya immediately sprang with her own words. Her eyes were almost on fire as she reminded him that everyone, including Frigg, knew of his heinous crime and that he was insane to even dredge those waters. Loki attacked Freya's promiscuous reputation and accused her of sleeping with every god and elf that had been gathered in the hall. She threatened to make Loki regret even coming to the party, but Loki would continue his accusations and said Freya had slept with her own brother.

This was too much for Njord to take because that was his daughter, and he told Loki that what she did behind closed doors was of no concern to anyone else. Loki would speak of the humiliating journey that Njord had been on after the Aesir-Vanir War to get to Asgard. Njord would admit that the journey was long, but he also would father his well-loved son and his beautiful daughter. Loki then cut through Njord's words by revealing that it was Njord's own sister that had birthed his children, and he added that at least he knew to expect his own children to share a bed too.

Poor Tyr would try to interject on behalf of Freyr. He would tell Loki how noble Freyr was and had avoided any scandalous activities, but Loki would be ready with another sly tongue lashing. He told Tyr that he had never been much of a "hand" at bringing two parties to a civil agreement and asked how it felt as his son bit off the god's hand. Tyr would remind Loki that his hand was a small price to pay since Fenrir would not be able to be at his father's side during Ragnarök. Loki would then tell Tyr that his wife was lucky to have been the mother to Loki's child and that Tyr was only paid one penny for the affair (this was only mentioned in "Lokasenna," so this reference is more dubious).

Freyr chimed in that Fenrir was tied down until the end of the world and threatened Loki that if he did not stop this abuse, he would meet the same fate. Loki could not wait for this, and he shamed Freyr for being so foolish and purchasing his own wife. He then reminded Freyr that because of his lovesick lunacy, he gave up his sword and would have to face the fire giants empty-handed.

Byggviir, Freyr's servant, was irate to hear his master disrespected in this way. He said if he was as brave as the god, he would take Loki and obliterate him. Loki would question who the yapping little creature was. After Byggvir introduced himself, Loki then assaulted him again by saying Byggvir was not much of a servant. This was followed by Loki telling him he spoke so bravely, yet anytime the gods were entrenched in battle, he was nowhere to be seen.

Heimdall then spoke up, but he would do so more calmly than the other gods. He told Loki that he was drunk of ale and rage and to just leave before he makes things worse. Loki would only yell at the watchman. Loki demeaned the god by telling him that his life was meaningless as he couldn't do anything but be the watchman of the gods.

Njord's wife, Skadi, would speak next, telling Loki that he was quick-witted but that it wouldn't matter when the gods tied him to a boulder with the insides taken from his dead son. Loki laughed and told Skadi that even if the gods did that, he still was the one who led the way when the gods killed her father Thiazi. Skadi would try to respond that her halls would curse Loki if he had really been responsible for her father's death. Loki then shut Skadi down by airing their secret relationship in front of all the guests.

Sif would get up and pour Loki a fresh cup of mead, and as she brought it to him, she asked that out of everyone there, he would surely find her innocent and spare her from his attacks. Perhaps this was to calm the trickster god, but it could have been to keep Sif's secret out of Loki's mouth. However, Loki was sparing no one on this night. He drank the mead and told Sif he would have loved to spare her, but he could not.

He then revealed that Sif's secret was that she had an affair with the trickster god. Sif would be speechless after that.

Beyla, Freyr's other servant, warned that the mountains were shaking and that meant Thor was on his way. Loki assaulted her by saying she had no place mixed up with the gods because she was an embarrassment.

By this point, Loki was so carried away that he did not see Thor enter the hall. Thor waited until he had finished his next round of vile assaults, and he slammed his fists on one of the tables. He demanded that Loki hold his tongue or risk being beheaded by Mjölnir. Loki responded by asking him how brave he was going to be as he would have to watch Fenrir swallow Odin whole. Again, Thor told him to be quiet or he would throw Loki so far east towards Jotunheim that no one would have to see him again. Loki responded by reminding Thor that his own journey east had seen Thor become a coward. Thor again threatened Loki with a punishment from Mjölnir, but Loki only could respond that he foresaw a long life ahead of him.

Thor's last threat was that he would use his hammer to send Loki to Hel. Suddenly, Loki was calm and wickedly smiling. He told Thor that he had shown the gods and goddesses just what he thought of them, but because of Thor, he would leave the hall. Loki knew how ill-tempered the god of thunder was and did not want to find out if his threats would come true.

Loki would pause and look around at all the shocked and angered faces of the guests. This brought him a brief moment of joy amid what was a horrible time for his own thoughts. Loki turned to Aegir, the last person to be addressed by Loki that night. He told the host that he made a very fine ale, but that ale and this feast would be the last that Aegir would ever host. He reminded him of what was to come and that his hall would be consumed by fire and his body would be burned during the approaching battle.

Loki took his leave of the feast, leaving only an echo of his cruel words. The gods, goddesses, and elves could do or say nothing. They only stared into their cups of ale for the longest time. Without saying a word, Aegir's guests stood up and, one by one, left the last feast they would ever have.

CHAPTER 6
THOR

Who is Thor?

There is no question that Thor is one of the most popular gods to come from Norse mythology. The son of Odin was the fiercest of the gods, and he could command lightning and thunder along with rain. That's why he's the thunder god. He would also rival Freya in promiscuity and is associated with fertility even today. We have seen the modern depiction of Thor, but he was originally depicted as having red hair and a red beard.

Thor embodies everything you think of when you think of a hero. He's brave, and powerful, stands up for what's good and righteous, and he's very hot-headed. Thor would turn to violence first as opposed to logic and reasoning. Yet, the gods would turn to him for many of their problems because he got the job done. Also, Odin was normally unavailable.

Thor is one of the oldest deities, as he was named in the first century when the Romans knew him as Jupiter. The most common relic uncovered from that region of the world is usually of Thor holding Mjölnir while in a seated position. Since then we have seen the legend of Thor still thriving today. His name does mean "thunder" in Old Norse, but Thor also had a few other names throughout history. Alti (the terrible), Björn (the bear), Einridi (the one who rides alone), Hardhugadr (braveheart), and

Vingthor (thunder hurler) have all been used at one point.

Yes, Thor was all the things a hero would need to be, but why did he do it? Thor believed in good, but just as Loki loved mischief, Thor loved being in a fight. There were rare moments that he would not fight. His prized possession was Mjölnir, the hammer given to him by the dwarves. The hammer could shoot lightning and crush his enemies. On some occasions, Mjölnir could even raise the dead.

What is often passed up in portrayals today is that he would wear iron gloves (Járngreipr) in order to carry the hammer. Another missed cosmetic was Megingjörd, a belt that doubled the strength Thor already had. He also had a staff, Grídarvölr, but this was rarely ever used.

Thor would often travel with Loki, but he mostly was accompanied by his twin servants, Thjálfi and Röskva. His chariot was pulled by Tanngrisnir and Tanngnjóstr, two goats that Thor would slaughter for food. Don't worry, he used Mjölnir to resurrect them each time. When Thor was in Asgard, his realm was in a Bilskirnir, a hall made of oak. This was allegedly the largest hall built in Asgard and had a total of 540 rooms!

Thor was half-giant, being born to Odin and Jord. Though he shared blood with the giants, they would be his greatest enemies. Because Odin fathered many children, Thor had a long list of half-brothers like Baldur, Váli, Vidarr, Tyr, Heimdall, Bragi, and Hodr.

Thor married Sif, the goddess associated with faith, family, and fertility. They had one daughter together, Thudr, who may have been one of the Valkyries. Another contradiction to his hatred of the giants was that his lover, Járnsaxa, was also a giant. They would have one son named Magni. He would have another son, Módi, from one of his countless affairs.

The Giant's Bride

One night, as Thor slept, a giant snuck into Asgard from Jotunheim and stole Mjölnir. Thor woke the next morning to the discovery and immediately flew into a fit of rage. Without that hammer, everyone was in danger. While Thor could argue that it left them in danger of an attack, it could have been his own anger that put them in danger. He only grew more irate as he searched for his prized possession.

He would understandably turn his attention to Loki because of the many misadventures he caused. Yet, the trickster was actually innocent this time. Loki would still provide some help and offered to go to Jotunheim to question the giants. Loki was using common sense this time since he could shapeshift and get answers.

Thor and Loki would turn to Freya for some help. She did, after all, have a cloak made of feathers that would give anyone that wore it the power of flight. Loki put the cloak on and set off for Jotunheim. As he arrived, he questioned the giants about the missing hammer.

He finally reached Thrym, a chief in Jotunheim. Loki got his answers, but not the answer that would please Thor. Thrym told him he stole the hammer and buried it far under the ground. He then added that he wouldn't think of returning the hammer until Freya would be his bride. After getting his answer, Loki flew back to Asgard to deliver the news.

There was no question that everyone was shocked and angry about what the giant had said. None angrier than Freya. Freya was a sight to behold and the giant was repulsive. This effectively killed the suggestion of Freya going to Jotunheim before it was even brought up. The gods would need to hold a council and come up with a plan.

Thor's half-brother, Heimdall, would be the one to come up with an idea. He suggested Thor go into Jotunheim dressed as Freya. If he did this, then he could recover Mjölnir and seek vengeance on those who stole it. Everyone loved the plan, and Loki even got a good laugh at the idea. Thor hated it. He argued that this was unfitting of a god, and it would be dishonorable and unmanly to dress as a goddess. He couldn't stomach the idea that he would be the laughing stock of Asgard. Loki quickly pointed out that if he didn't go with the plan, his hammer was gone and Asgard would be ruled by giants.

Begrudgingly, Thor agreed to Heimdall's idea. The gods then got to work assembling the wedding dress. Freya even loaned Thor her prized necklace so he could fit the part. Loki pulled the veil over Thor's face as he agreed to go with him under the disguise of Freya's servant. The two made their way to Jotunheim, and when they arrived, Thrym bragged he was finally getting what he was owed by marrying the lovely Freya.

That night, the giants would have a feast to celebrate Thrym's achievement and suspicion would be raised. Once again, it wasn't Loki's fault! While the gods took their time making a beautiful wedding dress, Thor forgot to work on his etiquette. He ate the food they had prepared for the "goddess." He also ate an ox and eight fish, and he drank multiple barrels of mead. Thrym noticed and remarked that he had never seen a woman with such an appetite. Thankfully, Loki was there and used his quick wit to save Thor. He claimed that "Freya" hadn't been able to eat because she was longing for over a week for her future husband.

It made sense to Thrym, so he accepted the answer. He had been waiting for his beloved Freya. He had the desire to kiss her, so he lifted the veil and his eyes met Thor's. Thor was glaring a hole into the giant which caused Thrym to make his surprising response. Loki, again, had to think fast. He told the giant that because she was longing for Thrym, she was unable to sleep for that entire week and it made her gaze fierce. Thrym accepted this answer as well.

Finally, it was time for the ceremony. To make their vows official, Thrym would call for Mjölnir to be raised. He laid the hammer down in

"Freya's" lap, and Thor took the hammer and killed Thrym first, followed by all the wedding guests. It was a bloody reception that wouldn't be rivaled until *Game of Thrones*. Thor returned to Asgard, changed clothes, and wouldn't let Mjölnir out of his sight again.

CHAPTER 7
FREYR

Who Was Freyr?

Freyr was a Vanir god who would be sent to Asgard after the Aesir-Vanir war. He was the god of peace and prosperity and was also associated with male virility, sunshine, and pleasant weather. Freyr and Freya were twins, and this meant that not only were they the most prominent of the Vanir, but they were both equally beautiful among the gods. Because of his charm and goodwill, he would become beloved and earn high praise from the Aesir as well.

While Freya would mean "lady," Freyr would equate to "lord." Because he was held in such high regard, Freyr would have many prized possessions. We saw that from the dwarves he had his enormous ship Skidbladnir and the golden boar, Gullinbursti. His last treasure was a sword that could fight on its own. Hopefully, he would never let that sword go.

Freyr's tree was the same as Freya's. She was his only sibling, and they were both sent to Asgard along with their father in the hostage exchange. There are no children that we know of, but he did have one wife, Gerdr.

When Freyr Met Gerdr

One day, while Odin was on another adventure, Freyr sat on Hlithskjalf. He could look across all nine realms, and he did so until his eyes fell on

Jotunheim. He saw Gymir's home and the mountains off to the side. It wasn't the house or the landscape that would capture his attention. Instead, it was a beautiful giantess. She walked up to the house and, before she entered, she lifted her arms. Her skin was so fair that light shined from them. It lit up the world and set Freyr's heart on fire.

As he walked away from Odin's throne, he fell into a deep depression. All he could think of was Gerdr, but he wouldn't tell anyone about it. He could have been afraid to admit that he sat on a throne he shouldn't have, or he could have been afraid of admitting that he had fallen in love with a girl from Jotunheim. The other gods saw his suffering, but none would speak to him. He quit drinking, eating, and sleeping because his heart ached so much.

His father, Njord, would become anxious about

his son. Instead of talking to him directly, though, he sent Freyr's servant Skirnir to find out what was wrong. It's not clear why Freyr trusted Skirnir with this delicate information, but he told the servant everything. Freyr would tell him that if he couldn't have the giantess, he had no reason to live.

After telling Skirnir everything, Freyr had the idea to send the servant to ask Gerdr to marry the Vanir god. He would give him a horse that could endure the flames around the giant's home, and he would pay him handsomely if he could achieve his goal. Skirnir agreed to the plan, but he wouldn't want riches as payment. He wanted Freyr's sword, and Freyr didn't hesitate. He gave up a sword that could fight on its own for a chance with Gerdr.

Skirnir then set out for Jotunheim to ask Gerdr to marry Freyr. He brought apples with him, and Gerdr could have them if she agreed to marry Freyr. With no hesitation of her own, she said no. Then he offered Draupnir, the golden ring the dwarves crafted for Odin. Again, Gerdr said no.

Skirnir then began to threaten the giantess. She didn't care at first because she did not want to marry Freyr. Then Skirnir threatened to put curses on her, and that eventually frightened her. She finally agreed to marry Freyr, but she told Skirnir that the god would have to wait nine days.

Freyr got what he wanted and still chose to mope over the next nine days. Let's not forget he gave up a sword. He would regret that decision after a while.

CHAPTER 8
IDUN

Who Was Idun?

Idun rarely gets a lot of recognition throughout Norse mythology, but she had one of the more important roles and one of the more famous myths even if she was in the background.

Idun was married to Bragi, a skald who was the narrator in sections of both of the Eddas. Her name roughly translates to "the young one" or "the rejuvenator."

The name was fitting as she had the power to reverse the aging effects of the gods. In her box made of ash, she carried her apples. Whenever the gods had started showing signs of aging, she would feed them the apples and the gods would be youthful again.

Not much is known about the goddess besides her family tree beside the fact she was married to Bragi. This likely is why Idun is not mentioned with higher regard.

The Abduction of Idun

Odin, Loki, and Hoenir were on a journey and found themselves in the mountains far from Asgard. With it being such a desolate area, food was scarce. The gods were starving, but they found relief when they found an ox herd. They quickly took to killing one in order to have dinner.

They made a fire and set the ox meat over it. However, the meat did not cook. They left it there for hours, but it remained raw. A voice called out to them. Looking around, they finally looked up and saw an eagle. The eagle told them that he had placed a spell on the area that prevented anyone from cooking meat unless the eagle was offered some in return. Naturally, the gods were irritated about a bird making demands of them, but they were hungry enough that a deal was made. The eagle flew down and ate the best parts of the ox meat. Loki was the most irate because he felt the eagle was being greedy, so he took a branch and swatted angrily at the eagle. The eagle took Loki in his talons and shot him into the sky. Loki was terrified. He begged the eagle to take him back, but what he didn't realize was that this was no ordinary eagle.

The eagle would turn out to be Thjazi, a giant who took disguise as a bird. He told Loki he would show mercy, but he had to bring him the youthful goddess, Idun, and her magical apples. With the other option being a long fall back to the ground, Loki swore an oath to the giant to bring him Idun and her fruit.

The giant took Loki back to Odin and Hoenir and the trio made their way back to Asgard. Loki quickly went to Idun and told her about the fruits he had seen on the journey. He told her she should grab her apples and go with him so they could compare the fruit. Idun chose to believe Loki. She grabbed her apples, and the two set off out of Asgard. They made it back to the mountains where Loki had made the deal, and Thjazi was waiting there in his eagle form. He swooped in and took the goddess in his talons up to his home, Thrymheim. This place was more desolate than the area below, but Loki had fulfilled his oath and went back home.

It wasn't long before everyone in Asgard would notice that Idun was gone. The gods and goddesses aged rapidly. They were wrinkled, grayed, and their energy had been depleted. Everyone would gather to find out what happened to Idun. This probably looked selfish, as it was their aging that made them concerned for the goddess. Someone had finally spoken up that Idun was last seen leaving with Loki. The gods quickly apprehended the trickster and threatened him just as Thor had done after his wife's hair was cut off. Loki spilled everything, being threatened if he didn't deliver Idun. The gods would respond by threatening his life if he didn't bring her home.

Freya would loan him the cloak again so he

could get to Thrymheim quickly, and Loki flew toward the Jotunheim palace. When he got there, he learned that Thjazi had gone fishing and left Idun all alone. It was a relief for Loki, and he got Idun and flew away in a hurry back to Asgard.

Maybe it was impeccable timing, but Thjazi returned shortly after and found that Idun was missing. He knew it could have only been one person to sneak in and steal her, so he took back his eagle form and flew off to Asgard. In a short amount of time, he was gaining on Loki. The gods saw the pursuit and set up kindling around the barrier. Loki made it just in time for the kindling to be ignited and that would be the end of Thjazi. Idun was safely at home in Asgard.

CHAPTER 9
HEIMDALL

Who Was Heimdall?

Heimdall was the watcher god who sat at the top of the Bifrost and would be the one who would sound the Gjallarhorn at the beginning of Ragnarök. He was suggested to be the guardian who would allow passage to and from the nine realms. He would grant knowledge and social status, which gave him high regard in Midgard.

Heimdall's name would translate to "radiant

world". He also had other names: Hallinskidi (the horned), Gullintanni (gold-toothed), Vindlér (the turner), and in the myth we will tell, Heimdall took the name Rígr.

In the *Prose Edda*, Heimdall would need very little sleep, could see in pitch black conditions with total clarity, and spot targets from over 300 miles away. He also had very sharp hearing abilities that would allow him to hear the grass grow. He didn't have many notable objects outside of the Gjallarhorn and his golden-maned horse, Gulltoppr. His castle, Himinbjörg, was at the Asgardian end of the rainbow bridge, so Heimdall worked close to home.

Heimdall was another son of Odin. His mothers were nine sea giants: Gjolp, Greip, Eistla, Eyrgjafa, Ulfrun, Angeyja, Imth, Atla, and Jarnsaxa (Thor's giantess love). Heimdall shared all the same half-brothers as Thor.

Heimdall had no wife and no lovers among giants or gods. However, he reproduced with Midgardians among three different classes of humans.

Heimdall's Midgard Adventure

There was a brief period where there was peace and tranquility throughout the nine realms. It was a golden age in Asgard, but this meant that Heimdall was very bored. Because of Gjallarhorn and his shiny presence, he couldn't go anywhere without being recognized and praised. Odin noticed not only was Heimdall getting listless, but he had been working for so long with no kind of break. He knew that all was well in Asgard, so he told the watchman to take some time and go on an adventure of his own. He told Heimdall that he would wear disguises as he journeyed the nine realms.

That was all Heimdall needed to hear because he

had been wanting to visit the humans in Midgard for so long. He put his horn and sword aside, disguised himself as a human, and traveled down the Bifrost to a beach in Midgard.

The first people he would meet were Edda and Ai, a struggling couple that was barely surviving life on the beach. Their house was in shambles, and they had virtually nothing to their name. However, they offered their meager seaweed bed to the traveler. He squeezed between the couple and slept peacefully.

After three nights, Heimdall asked the couple to join him. He had gathered pieces of driftwood, and the couple watched as he made a pointed stick from one and cut a hole in the other. He placed the pointed stick into the other piece of driftwood and rubbed them together until the wood began to smolder. A fire soon started, and the couple were left in awe of this "magic" they witnessed. Heimdall thanked them for what they had done for him and set off to venture more.

Ai and Edda saw their entire lives transform because of this gift, but the fire wasn't the only gift Heimdall had left. Nine months later, Thrall was born. Thrall would go on to marry Serf and have many children who worked as hard as their parents did. Thus, Heimdall was the father of the thralls.

After leaving the beach couple, Heimdall would arrive at the house of Amma and Afi. He noticed that Afi was whittling away at beams to make improvements to their home. Heimdall set his things down and began to help. Soon, they had made a magnificent loom that they would give to Amma. He was thankful for the help, and she was thankful for the gift. Therefore, they offered Heimdall a place to sleep in between them. Nine months after he left their home, Amma gave birth to Karl the Yeoman. He was a beautiful boy who loved the land so much that he wanted to make it even more beautiful. Karl would marry a woman that made sure their house ran smoothly as he worked. They, too, had many children, which made Heimdall the father of the Bondi, the yeoman farmers.

His third visit was to a castle belonging to a very wealthy couple. The man spent his time crafting his bow and spears for hunting while the wife sat by his side. They offered the same kindness to Heimdall. He was fed delicious food and offered a place between them in their bed. Heimdall didn't want to leave, but he knew he would need to resume his duties. He would leave the couple with a gift, and nine months later, Jarl the Earl was born. Jarl would learn to hunt and live off the land as his father did, and he would get his refined nature and beauty from his mother. He would be known to others as "Regal," and when Regal was a boy, Heimdall returned to claim his son. Even though the boy remained in Midgard, the world soon learned who his father was and he grew to be their ruler. He married Erna and had many more sons including another named Jarl. This made Heimdall the father of the nobles and kings that would rule the lands for all time.

CHAPTER 10
TYR

Who Was Tyr?

Not much is known about Tyr. For the Germanic people, he was one of the oldest gods. Because of our lack of information, Tyr is either the god of war and bloodshed or he is the bringer of order and justice.

Either would work, but given the myth that he is most tied to, Tyr was really a god of justice and possibly the most righteous of the gods. While he knew that the wolf Fenrir was going to be a problem later on for the gods, he still raised the wolf from a pup and had a feeling that he was betraying the trust of Fenrir when the gods ordered the wolf to be bound. He knew the price of trapping the wolf and was the only one to pay it. This is how Tyr would become the one-handed god.

Tyr was either the son of Odin or the son of Hymir. At the beginning of Aegir's feast for the gods, they had run out of mead. Aegir would brew ale for the gods if they could get him a massive cauldron. This is when Tyr would announce that his father was the giant Hymir and had the right-sized cauldron for the ale. This was the only myth that had Tyr fathered by someone else, and the god even disappears for much of the story.

The Binding of Fenrir

All three of Loki's children with Angrboda would have their own role in the downfall of the Aesir. Jormungandr was cast out to the sea around Midgard by Odin while Hel was sent to Niflheim (or Hel) to reign over the dead.

The child that worried the gods most, though, was the giant wolf Fenrir. Fenrir was prophesied to bring death to Odin during Ragnarök, but the gods felt they could change the fate. They believed that if the wolf were to remain wild and free, he would surely become the monster they were warned of. They were desperate to avoid this situation, so they would come up with the idea that if they raised the wolf instead, he would not become the bringer of the Allfather's death.

They brought the pup to Asgard, but none of the gods wanted to do anything to raise Fenrir. It was only Tyr that was brave enough to approach Fenrir. The gods were too afraid of the wolf's power and his massive size even as a pup, so it became Tyr's job to feed and raise him. Time would pass and Fenrir continued to grow and become a size that even Tyr was afraid of. They did build a bond, however, so there was still a trust developed between god and wolf. However, it was at this point the gods knew that the giant wolf needed to be restrained.

The gods began to play a "game" with Fenrir. They would trap him and tie him down, and each time, the wolf would break free. Fenrir was a happy pup and enjoyed winning the game against the gods, but the gods grew increasingly worried. It didn't matter what bounds they used to trap the wolf, Fenrir would break free.

The gods then used the heaviest iron they could find called Laeding. They approached Fenrir and challenged him to test his strength. They knew that if Fenrir couldn't break the restraints, they would leave him tied down forever. All of them had underestimated the wolf's strength, and they watched as Fenrir shattered the iron with no effort at all.

They tried making new restraints on their own. They came up with something thicker and stronger than the iron and called it Dromi. Again, Fenrir broke the restraints with no effort, and enjoyed this increased challenge in the "game." He waited eagerly for the gods to bring his next challenge.

What Fenrir did not realize was that the gods were now desperate. Fenrir was too strong and he needed to be restrained. The gods would send a messenger to the dwarves to make a new restraint. The dwarves sent back Gleipnir—made from the sound a cat makes when it moves, the beard of a woman, roots of a mountain, fibers made from bear tendons, fish breath, and the spit of a bird. Gleipnir looked like a thin cord compared to the heavy-looking chains the gods had used before.

Fenrir was immediately suspicious that the gods were trying to trick him. He suspected they were using magic or something else to cheat at their "game." The gods tried to reason with the wolf and told him that they would let him go if he wasn't able to break the restraints. Fenrir wasn't hearing it and demanded that one of the gods put his hand in the wolf's mouth before he was restrained again. It was a good faith clause implemented by the wolf.

The gods knew that if he could not break free, he would be bound forever, so they were all hesitant to put any part of their body in the wolf's mouth. The only one brave enough was

Tyr, the god who had raised Fenrir. This would be good enough for the wolf, and he agreed to be restrained.

While the other restraints required no effort at all, Gleipnir proved to be stronger than Fenrir had realized. He struggled to break free as he held Tyr's hand in his mouth. The other gods laughed as they realized their plan was finally working. Besides the restraints, this really angered the wolf.

While Tyr was the only one to offer his hand, it may have been because he felt it was honorable to the wolf. Tyr had raised the pup, and there was a bond between the two. Tyr knew it was necessary since this was the being that would kill Odin, but he couldn't help but feel as if he was betraying Fenrir. He remained calm even as Fenrir admitted defeat.

It was then the wolf realized the gods had no intentions of letting him go, and Fenrir's rage exploded. He bit down on Tyr's hand and swallowed it. While he was still bound, he took his payment in the form of Tyr's flesh. The gods got more of a laugh as they finally restrained the magnificent wolf. Everyone laughed except Tyr. Tyr not only lost his hand, but he betrayed Fenrir. The gods then took a sword and placed it vertically in the wolf's mouth so he could no longer howl. They took Fenrir to an island and bound him to a rock where he would remain until Ragnarök, when he would finally break free and exact his revenge on the leader of the gods.

While on the island, Hati and Sköll tried to free their father, but they couldn't break free from the wolf's restraints. Hati and Sköll would go on to devour the moon and the sun during Ragnarök.

CHAPTER 11
FRIGG

Who Was Frigg?

The goddess of motherhood and fertility, Frigg was the queen of the gods. Frigg also ruled over other areas of life, such as marriage, love, sexuality, wisdom, and prophecy. Again, Frigg and Freya could easily be the same person. It is a "have you seen Frigg and Freya in the same room?" situation. It could be that this one goddess had a split personality because Freya acted as the other gods did by having lovers across the realms, but Frigg was portrayed as being more moral in that sense. Again, we will leave them as separate entities.

Frigg's name would mean "beloved, dear." As Odin's wife, Frigg would get to sit next to the Allfather. She was the only goddess to have that right. Odin and Frigg would be parents to Hermod and Baldur.

Agnar and Geirrod

Hrauthung, a great king, had two sons, Agnar (10) and Geirröth (8). The boys were warned to never go out alone, but one day they decided to take a boat so they could go fishing. A storm developed, and the boys couldn't escape it. Their boat was pulled out far into the sea and pushed to an unknown shore. The boys were stranded and scared, but they were soon found by a peasant couple. The man took care of Geirröth while the woman tended to Agnar. After some time, the man would send Geirröth back to his home. Once he arrived, he learned that his father had passed, but the people were excited as the rightful successor to the throne returned.

Meanwhile, Odin and Frigg were watching from their thrones in Asgard. They took interest in the children because the peasants who rescued them were none other than Odin and Frigg. Odin then would brag to Frigg that the child he took care of was now a king. He would also mock the fact that Agnar was married and having children with a giantess. Basically, Odin was slandering Frigg's motherhood abilities.

Frigg wouldn't stand for Odin's dismissal of Agnar. She fired back that while Geirröth was king, he wasn't very fitting for the title. She pointed out how cruel he was to his guests and his subjects, but Odin would disagree with her. It was then that Odin and Frigg would make a bet to see who was the better parent. Odin would shapeshift into a traveler and try to visit with the king. They would then learn who should do the slandering. Frigg was not about to lose the bet, so she would send someone to deliver a message to Geirröth. The message would tell the king that a wizard would soon be there to try to bewitch him.

Odin soon arrived in the kingdom and wanted to visit with the king he had taken care of as a lost boy. Geirröth wanted to know what the traveler's business was, but Odin only told him his name was Grimnir. He gave the name and nothing more. This would raise the king's suspicion that the traveler was the wizard that he was warned of. Geirröth ordered that the traveler be placed between two fires, and that was where the so-called "Grimnir" would sit for eight nights. Eventually, the king's youngest son brought Grimnir some ale, and from that, Grimnir would tell the boy a story that would become the rest of "The Ballad of Grimnir"

(Grímnismál).

Once Grimnir revealed he was Odin, Geirröth tried to attack him out of his own fear. The king was far too flustered and fell on his sword, dying instantly. Odin disappeared back to Asgard and watched the far kinder Agnar take the throne. This proved him wrong, and Frigg won the bet.

CHAPTER 12
BALDUR

Who Was Baldur?

The last of the key figures is Baldur, the son of Odin and Frigg. Baldur was the most beloved of the gods and was only rivaled in his beauty by Freyr and Freya. Even then, he would rise above the twins because his beauty caused him to actually radiate light. He was also the wisest of the gods, and would aid in the disputes of gods and men. Baldur was seen as an ideal god in Norse mythology, and it's what makes his timeline the saddest.

Not known for being a god of battle meant that his most notable attributes were fairness, beauty, and likeability. Everyone loved Baldur. While Freyr's ship was majestic, Baldur's was undoubtedly better. The Hringhorni was said to be the greatest ship ever built, and Baldur loved it so much that it would become his pyre in death. His horse, Léttfeti, would be sacrificed on his pyre as well. Finally, his palace, Breidablik, was said to be the most peaceful palace by Odin himself.

Baldur had one brother from Odin and Frigg's marriage, Hodr. This also meant that Baldur had many half-brothers because of the Allfather. One of those half-brothers, Váli, was conceived by Odin and the giantess Rindr after Baldur's death. Váli only had one purpose, and it was avenging his brother's death. Baldur would marry the goddess Nanna and would have one son, Forseti. Forseti would become the god of peace and justice.

The Death of Baldur

More and more, Baldur's sleep was being invaded by ominous bad dreams. They would speak of a fatal misfortune that would come to the most beloved god. Because of his standing with the gods, they asked Odin to go and find out what all of Baldur's dreams meant. Odin disguised himself and journeyed to the underworld to find a dead seeress. He looked for her because these types of prophecies were her specialty.

When he reached the underworld, he noticed the halls were decorated, and it looked like they were planning some type of feast or party. He finally found the seeress and immediately questioned her about what was going on. She replied they were having a special guest soon and it would be none other than Baldur. Odin was horrified, but the seeress continued by telling him how Baldur would die. She was excited because all that came to the underworld would then serve under Loki's daughter, Hel, which meant that they would now have a powerful god in their ranks. Her joy would soon pass when she realized who she was talking to.

Odin returned home in sadness. He told the gods what he learned and Frigg was devastated. They would then discuss all the ways someone could die, and Frigg would take heed of all the ways to die. No matter how slim the chances were, Frigg was going to journey to all nine realms to get every living and nonliving thing to take an oath to not harm her precious son.

Fire and water would swear their oath along with every metal. The stones and rocks came next and they swore the same oath. The earth and the trees joined in, followed by every type of illness. Every animal, giant, human, elf, and dwarf would swear to never harm Baldur. Her mission was long, but soon she had everything sworn to never hurt him.

Frigg returned to Asgard, and the gods and goddesses wanted to verify that Baldur was protected. One picked up a pebble and threw it right at Baldur's head, but Baldur felt nothing. Apparently, it had worked, and Frigg could breathe in relief that Baldur was safe.

The gods and goddesses would hold a daily councils to discuss the feats of the humans on Midgard. After they talked about business, they simply enjoyed being in the company of other gods. They would drink, sing, perform tests of strength, and would even play games such as chess. The one pebble would soon turn into their new favorite game. It started out with just pebbles, but the rocks got larger. Baldur boasted because he felt nothing.

This had become the game of "let's try to kill Baldur," and it was all the gods wanted to do. They began throwing the sharpest darts they had at Baldur. Other gods brought stones now to hurl at him, but everything would bounce off of him. It was as if his skin was stone itself. The other gods would try to swing their axes, swords, and any weapon they had, and watch in amusement as Baldur's skin resisted all of it. He was immortal. Baldur was now the victim of the most violent attacks, but he and the gods enjoyed this new game because no one got hurt. The god and game were loved by all.

That was except for Loki, who despised the gods for how he was treated by the dwarves in Asgard so long before. He had more reason to hate them now as he watched the precious Baldur absorb these attacks and never show a scratch. He was sickened by this boastful act, but he couldn't stop watching. Surely, there had to be something that would take Baldur down, and he knew just who to ask.

One day, as the gods played their game of "attempted murder," Loki slipped away. He would shape-shift into an old woman and begin walking the halls of Asgard. He approached Frigg's hall, and as he hoped, she was all alone. Frigg saw this old woman and rose to greet her. Frigg listened as the woman explained how she came across a violent act where this beautiful man was being stoned and stabbed. The old woman reckoned that the man must be dead by now since no one could endure that kind of abuse.

Frigg waited until she was done and reassured the woman that she had not witnessed a barbaric act. She explained that since her son could no longer be hurt, the gods had made it a game to at least try. The woman questioned her about what type of magic it was, and Frigg explained that everything took an oath to never hurt her son.

The questions the woman asked only made Frigg repeat everything took an oath. It must have finally worn the goddess down because she told the woman that the young mistletoe did not swear an oath, but it was still so young that it couldn't cause any harm. The woman said she had to go, and Frigg was not upset by this.

Once he left the hall, he shifted back to Loki and had a trot to his step as he went back across the plains of Idavoll. He continued further west, past the gods, and Baldur still playing their game. Finally, he found what he was looking for growth from the trunk of a tree. Loki had just found the mistletoe that would finally show Baldur could get hurt. What Loki didn't know was just how much it would hurt. He grabbed the bush and pulled it from the tree, picking off the berries and leaves as he headed back to the gods. He finally found a branch that was as long as his arm and began to whittle one end until it was a sharp point.

Loki had finished his work as he reached Gladsheim, the area where the gods gathered for their council. The gods were still playing and were so focused on the game that they did not see Loki leave. Loki gazed across the hall, noticing that everyone was there now, including Frigg. He also noticed Baldur's blind brother, Hodr, standing off to the side. Every time a dart, sword, or stone hit Baldur, Hodr would convulse in either laughter or sadness.

The trickster god then gulped down a glass of

wine and walked over to the lonely Hodr. Loki asked him why he wasn't playing the game with the other gods. The answer was obvious, but Hodr told Loki he wasn't playing because he could not see where Baldur stood. At first, Loki tried to play to the sentiment that they were excluding the god. Hodr would tell him that being jealous and vengeful was never the answer. Loki could see that he was affected, however, he was bitter about not joining. Hodr asked what the cheers were for, and Loki responded by telling him what he had seen.

Once again, he suggested to Hodr that he should play at least once. Hodr tried to object, saying he had no weapon. Of course, this was Loki's opening as he offered him the sharpened branch of mistletoe. Loki then offered to stand behind Hodr and guide him so that he could finally be part of the fun. He knew his plan was working, which only made Loki that much more desperate to see the result.

Loki guided Hodr's arm until it was aimed at Baldur. The branch flew, and Hodr waited for the laughter. Surely there would be laughter. Either they would laugh at another deflection or at Hodr's wild miss. The hall fell silent. That one branch of mistletoe had hit Baldur, but continued through Baldur. The beautiful god fell face-first to the hall floor. He was dead instantly.

The gods were silent and still. They couldn't even move Baldur's body to check. They already knew he was dead. Their shocked gaze turned to an accusing one as they panned to the spot Hodr and Loki stood. They already knew the only person who could be that malicious was Loki. This was not the moment to exact revenge, though, and the gods remained in place. The fact Loki hung his head and slinked out of the hall into the darkness may tell us that he wanted to hurt Baldur, but his prank had once again gone too far.

Once Loki was gone, the silence was broken by the sound of a goddess crying out. One by one, all the gods wept. They could only cry over the loss of Baldur. Odin was there as well and knew that this was the greatest evil and the events that were soon to follow.

A Mission and The Funeral

The first to speak was Frigg. She asked if anyone would ride down to Hel to find Baldur. The goddesses answered by crying once again. Frigg once again asked and added that she wanted someone to ride to the underworld and ask what the goddess Hel would want for letting Baldur go.

Odin's son Hermod, who was known for his boldness, offered to go on behalf of Asgard.

Voices filled the air as everyone was planning Hermod's trip down. Odin called for Sleipnir to be brought forward. The Allfather then took the reins and handed them to Hermod. The god looked out on the sad faces of the gods and goddesses who were still mourning for Baldur and set off for the underworld.

Gods and goddesses alike did not sleep. Instead, they held a silent vigil around the body of the fallen god. They thought that what had happened was going to bring Ragnarök, so they knew it was time to question their mortality. All of them thought of Hermod, hoping he could bring Baldur home. They thought of what they were going to do to Hodr and Loki for punishment. It had been Loki's doing that brought about Baldur's death, but it had been Hodr's hand that held the branch.

The day would break, and Asgard was greeted by

lightning in the east. It would soon spread in every direction, and the gods grew more fearful of what would come next. Four gods lifted Baldur, the others formed a procession behind them, and they walked the body down to Baldur's ship. The Hringhorni would serve as a pyre fit for a god of Baldur's stature. They tried to move the ship themselves, but grief had caused them all to be exhausted and unable to make the ship budge.

The gods sent a message to Jotunheim to ask for help. Help would come in the form of Hyrrokkin. Her strength was that of Asgard's finest, and she would soon come upon a wolf with vipers as reins. Odin would send four guards to watch over the wolf, which became angered at the sight of gods. A battle would ensue, and the guards would eventually beat the wolf down and leave it for dead. Hyrrokkin paid no mind as she made her way to the ship. She dug her heels in and pulled on the ship.

Hyrrokkin was so strong that the ship raced down into the water with enough force to cause all nine realms to tremble.

Thor, already upset about her wolf, took this as a sign of disrespect from Hyrrokkin. He threatened to kill her, but Odin told him to ignore it as there had already been enough bloodshed. The gods picked Baldur's body back up, walked it down, and laid it upon his ship. As his body passed, Nanna's heart would break, killing her. Her body would be laid next to her husband's on the ship.

Before the ceremony began, a large gathering made their way to the seaside: gods, goddesses, both Aesir and Vanir, the Valkyries, light elves, dwarves, and giants. The pyre was built and gifts were laid on the ship by anyone who chose to. Baldur's horse was killed and set on the ship as well. Odin was the last god to be on the ship. He took Draupnir, his prized golden ring, and laid it on Baldur's body. The Allfather stepped off and signaled for the pyre to be lit. Thor raised his hammer and hallowed the ceremony. The ship was released and sailed off with the flames growing higher. Everyone at this point knew what was coming unless a miracle happened.

The Prelude

Meanwhile, Hermod rode for nine long nights further down on his quest to rescue Baldur, who had been sent to Hel. He arrived at the river Gjoll which was guarded by the giantess Modgud. She asked his name and purpose, noting that it was strange that he made the sound of an army as only one man. She also pointed out that Hermod didn't appear to be dead. He answered honestly, and Modgud remembered when Odin had been there before to visit the seeress. Both her memory and his answer were to her satisfaction, and she allowed him to finish his journey.

He reached the towering walls of Hel's hall, Eljudnir. With one bound, Sleipnir jumped over the iron gates and led Hermod inside. After he dismounted, he walked through the hall, looking into the endless sea of dead faces. He would break his gaze from there as he saw Baldur sitting in the seat next to Hel's throne. Baldur was pale, and sad, but remained untouched.

Hel was deep in sleep by the time Hermod arrived, but he waited all night in the hall. Hel awoke and took her place on her throne while noticing that Hermod was there. He approached her and told her that there had been a mistake. All of Asgard was now in mourning and they needed their beloved Baldur back. Hel listened to all of Hermod's carefully chosen words, never once changing her expression.

Hermod had finished, and Hel would question him. She did not believe that Baldur was that loved. She probably knew her father well at that point, but that was never clearly said. However, she did humor Hermod with her offer. She told him that if everything in the nine realms cried for the beautiful god, she would let him go. She would emphasize that if there was a single thing that shed no tears, Baldur would stay there forever.

Hel allowed Baldur and his wife, Nanna, to accompany Hermod out of the hall. They walked him to the gate, still pale, still in a state of sadness. Baldur gave Hermod the golden ring, Draupnir, to give back to his father. Nanna took her headdress and other gifts to be given to Frigg. Hermod would honor the god and goddess and assured them they would soon return to Asgard. The entire universe was affected by his death, and they would all surely cry for him.

Hermod set off back to Asgard. He was greeted with hopeful looks, and he told the gods and goddesses what he had seen and the ransom price that Hel had set. The Aesir wasted no time sending messengers across all nine realms to shed tears for the fallen god and release him from Hel's side.

All the elements that swore oaths to Frigg were the first to cry. Next were all the animals of the land, the birds, and the insects—all cried for Baldur. Even the winds and weather wept, and the messengers were hopeful as they got all of Jotunheim to cry as well. They made their way back to Asgard, confident that they had accomplished their mission. Their hopes would soon be gone as they found a cave between Jotunheim and Asgard. This was the home of a giantess named Thokk.

The messengers told Thokk of their need so they could bring Baldur back from the underworld. Thokk would give them an answer that would dash all hopes to avoid Ragnarök. She told them she could and would not cry for Baldur because she did not care for him alive, nor did she care for him dead. They pleaded and begged the giantess to shed a tear, but she held her ground. She told them to let Hel hold what she has.

Those messengers then made the saddest journey back home to Asgard. The gods waited eagerly at the other end of the Bifrost, but they knew as soon as they saw the messengers that the news was grim. Gods and goddesses alike were devastated. They now had to accept that they could only mourn Baldur, but they also had to accept the chain of events that were soon to come. The last thing they had to accept was that the giantess in the cave was not Thokk. It was Loki in disguise, and he had no regret for what he had done.

CHAPTER 13
THE TWILIGHT OF
THE GODS

Except for Tyr, who only appeared a couple of times in the myths, we have met all the key characters in Norse mythology and told some of the stories that they were involved in. But just as there was a beginning, there was an end. After Baldur's death, the wheels would then be in motion to take the gods to the end of their time.

Before we finish the timeline of the gods, we will discuss the fate of Hodr. There was no doubt that Hodr held the branch that killed his brother, but what would become of him differed in separate tellings. In one, he was a great warrior that would be one of the survivors of Ragnarök and fought alongside his brother in the great battle. In the *Prose Edda*, Odin's son Vali would be born and within his first day of existence would grow to full size and kill Hodr. For our Ragnarök, we will use Snorri's version of Hodr's fate because he should have known better than to trust Loki.

The Binding of Loki

After Baldur was gone, Loki knew he would never be allowed in Asgard again. He slinked away from the piercing gaze of the Aesir gods and never returned. While it was unclear whether he truly intended for Baldur to die, he still hated the beautiful god. He went as far as disguising himself as a giantess and refused to cry to release Baldur from the underworld.

While the gods were in mourning for Baldur, Loki had run away to a mountain. From his new cave fortress called Fránangr, he could see out in all directions of any incoming attacks. He knew this was effortless and the gods would catch him one day, but he remained there.

With the mourning period over, Odin could take his place on Hlidskjálf, which allowed him to see *everything*, including where Loki was hiding. He then sent the Aesir out to apprehend the trickster god. Loki saw them coming, burned his own fishing nets, and jumped into the river, taking the shape of a fish in order to escape.

The gods arrived, saw the burned fishing nets, and could only assume that Loki did this because he was now a fish in the river. They would make their own net and cast it out, but they failed the first time because Loki would swim under it. They weighed the net down and cast it out again, but Loki would jump over it. The gods then split up in order to flank Loki. As he saw Thor coming up the river, Loki had to choose. He could swim out into the open sea or he could jump the net again. He jumped the net, but this time he was snatched out of the air by Thor.

Loki was taken into a cave, and the gods would exact their vengeance. The second group had gone after Loki was captured to find Loki's children, Vali and Narvi. They changed Vali into a wolf and immediately Vali pounced on Narvi. Vali would brutally murder his brother in front of Loki and take off to Jotunheim after.

Loki was broken and hopeless. The gods then

threw him to the ground, and Loki never fought back. They grabbed three massive rocks and lay Loki over them. They would then take the entrails of Narvi and bind Loki to the rocks. Almost immediately, the entrails became hard as iron. The gods then brought an enormous snake into the cave and braced it against the cave's ceiling. The snake was positioned just right so that the venom would drip onto Loki's face. Loki was left to think of how the gods had just left him there, and he became sorrowful. All he had was his wife, Sigyn. The couple were broken-hearted at seeing what happened to their sons. Sigyn remained loyal to Loki, however, and she would hold a bowl over Loki's head to catch the venom. However, the bowl would get full, and every time she would leave to empty it, venom would drip onto Loki's face.

Each time the venom would hit his skin, Loki would writhe in pain. With each tremble, the world would tremble as well. This is where Loki would remain until Ragnarök.

Ragnarök

It was fated to happen, but the death of Baldur was to be the first event to set off the chain reaction. The next was the release of Loki from his bindings. Whether it was because he could never return or fueled by blind rage towards the gods, he would side with the giants and his daughter, Hel.

There would be four ages before the world would meet its end: an ax-age, a sword-age, wind-age, and a wolf-age. In Midgard, there would be a bloody and massive war for three winters. It would be a lawless time and countless would be lost. Fimbulvetr, the winter to beat all winters, will set in. Midgard would be caught in the bitter wind and frost, and humanity would have to endure three more winters afterward with no warmth in between for relief.

In the sky, Sköll would finally catch Sol and devour her while covering the cosmos in her blood. Hati would outpace Mani, the moon, and finish him before he could recover. The stars would then vanish from the sky. Earth would then succumb to a massive earthquake that would topple mountains and flatten forests. From that earthquake, the great wolf Fenrir would run free again after being imprisoned by Tyr.

In Jotunheim, the watchman of the giants, Eggther, played his harp. He had a grim smile. The giants were going to war with the gods, but he knew there was no favorable outcome on either side. Three roosters then crowed to signal the beginning of Ragnarök itself.

Fjalar, a red rooster, called to the land of the giants. A golden-colored Gullinkambi who normally woke the warriors in Valhalla called to the gods. An unnamed rust-red rooster cawed and raised the dead in Hel.

Jormungandr, the sea serpent of Midgard began to twist and writhe as he furiously tried to get on dry land. His writhing pummeled the shorelines with unfathomable waves. Those waves broke Naglfar, the ship made with dead men's nails, free, and it would be filled to capacity with giants. They were making their way to the plains of Vigrid, the battleground where the war would take place. Loki would ride alongside the giants with Hel and her army.

Fenrir and Jörmungandr made their way to Vigrid. Flames from Fenrir's nostrils scorched the ground, and the venom from Jörmungandr's mouth would pollute the same earth and the sky.

The sound of quakes and booms filled the air, and from the south, the fire giants made their way from Muspellheim. Surtr and his flaming sword tore apart the sky and scorched all in his path. The sons of Muspellheim would join the giants, Loki and Hel's army of the dead, and Fenrir and Jormungandr. They lined one side of Vigrid's plains and awaited their foes.

The gods saw what was happening and knew it was time for their last great battle. Heimdall left his hall and blew the Gjallarhorn, and the sound traveled across all nine realms. The gods were signaling to themselves that this was Ragnarök. They met at once and held one last council. Odin left to gain one last piece of advice from Mimir's well.

Yggdrasil knew that this was going to be a universal reset, and the tree let out a moan as its leaves shook. Everything within the nine realms shook in kind. Two humans took refuge deep inside the tree, bracing for the impending war.

The side of the gods would all arm themselves. Aesir, Vanir, and the warriors who crossed to Valhalla would get swords, shields, or spears, and they would put on the armor that hopefully would withstand the attacks. With Odin leading the way, the vast army of the gods made their way to Vigrid.

Both sides eyed their opposition and made their battle claims. Odin made his way to Fenrir. Thor tried to ride next to Odin but was immediately attacked by Jormungandr. Freyr made his way to the fire giant, Surtr, but would be no match. Surtr had his great flaming sword that was setting fire to anything it touched. Freyr *would* regret that he gave his own blade up in his pursuit of Gerdr. The battle between them would be long, but Freyr could not beat the giant. The massive hound, Garm, would leap at the rarely mentioned Tyr, and they would kill each other almost instantly.

Loki and Heimdall would meet. The lifetime of anger flew out of Loki and the fierce defensiveness of Heimdall led to an intense battle. Both of them would shapeshift into the forms of seals and fight to the death. Neither of them would survive, so arguably, both of their fates were sealed. There is still a place in Ragnarök for bad jokes.

Thor and Jormungandr had met already, and this would prove to be a brutal fight. Thor slew the serpent who had threatened his beloved Midgard, but he would succumb to the serpent's venom. Odin and Fenrir were still in their own fierce battle, but eventually, the giant wolf would get hold of the Allfather and swallow him whole. The leader of the gods was now dead. His son Vidar would lunge at the wolf. Placing one foot on the bottom of Fenrir's jaw, Vidar pulled up on the wolf's head. Fenrir has ripped apart just as he'd gotten the most devastating kill in the war.

After defeating Freyr, Surtr would use his sword to toss fire in every direction. All nine realms were set on fire, leaving them all in ashes. Gods, humans, elves, dwarves, giants, all the dead in the underworld, animals, and creatures would all perish. The sun and moon were gone, and all the stars in the sky had been extinguished. That magnificent earth that the gods had carefully made from Ymir's body would sink into the sea. The war was over, just as it had been predicted.

New Beginning

Odin's sons, Vidar and Vali, would survive the fire and flood. They watched as Midgard emerged, lusher than it had been before. The boys made their way back to Idavoll, and they were joined by Modi and Magni, the sons of Thor. Modi and Magni would inherit Mjölnir. Baldur and Hodr would return from the land of the dead.

Grass soon returned to Idavoll. Beauty was returning. Hoenir survived, after all, that time and would tell the remaining gods what was to be for the future. Odin's brothers, Vili and Ve, had children as well, and they would join the new gods. They all told of the memories they had, beginning the oral tradition that would pass down over time.

Palaces would once again rise in place of the ones that had been there in the times of the old gods. The most breathtaking thing the gods witnessed was Lif and Lifthrasir emerging from Yggdrasil and taking their place in Midgard. They had managed to survive the fires and the flood as well, and they survived on dew alone. They see new light as Sol's daughter took her mother's place in the sky.

The humans would have children, and those children would help replenish the life on earth that had perished long ago. It was a new beginning, but the gods knew that eventually, this meant that Ragnarök would come again.

CHAPTER 14
NORSE MYTHOLOGY
AND POP CULTURE

The last chapter was not the happiest of times, but without creation and Ragnarök, we wouldn't have the mythology we have today. It is fascinating to read on its own, but more so is how those myths are referenced in pop culture. From books and games to music and television, Norse characters and their stories seem to find their way to us through different media, and it would be impossible to name them all here. That would need another book on its own! This chapter is just some favorites of one of the HBA's teams of enthusiasts.

The MCU

One of the most notable calls to Norse mythology is none other than the Marvel Cinematic Universe (MCU). Thor's story had been referenced before, but the MCU became a global phenomenon. How much did they reference and how accurate was it?

First, we will start with the Allfather, the god of wisdom, war, poetry, and many others. In the Marvel universe, Odin is severely underpowered and under-appreciated. For an actor like Anthony Hopkins, he is underpowered. The MCU portrays Odin as a calm figure who doesn't say or do much at all and is more of an old king living his last days. He *is* married to Frigg, but they list his children as Thor, Loki, and Hela (Hel). In mythology, Loki was more of a step-brother to Odin, and Hel was Loki's daughter. While Hopkins made a great interpretation and portrayal of an "Odin" figure, it was not accurate to the original tales.

Thor is actually more accurate than some would like to admit. The largest difference is that the ginger god in Norse mythology is a far cry from Chris Hemsworth's golden locks. MCU keeps him as the god of thunder and as a protector of Midgard, but as for his other associations in mythology, they are absent. Thor's temperament is largely the same in the movies as mythology would tell us. Thor was a hot-headed god and always ready for a fight. Of course, Jane Foster was a complete fabrication, though it would be hard to argue that Thor had lovers in Midgard as well. His wife, Sif, was only another war god in the movies and not his wife. They gave a nod to mythology in the *Loki* series when Sif reminds Loki that he cut off her hair. MCU left out the belt that increased his strength, but that could easily be looked over. They did, however, change that Thor needed special gloves to wield Mjölnir to the need to be "worthy" of the hammer. While it missed with accuracy, it made for a glorious moment when Captain America wielded the hammer in *Avengers: Endgame.*

The next notable MCU character was the trickster god Loki. Tom Hiddleston did an exceptional job nailing down Loki's silver-tongued abilities. They also portrayed the different sides of Loki as a helpful god who would get the Aesir out of trouble to the deviant who couldn't resist getting in trouble. You loved him, and you hated him, which was a prevalent theme in Norse mythology. MCU embellished him, of course, but the character was fairly accurate.

Idris Elba would give a different physical model

to the Heimdall that existed in the myths, but his portrayal of the Norse god was the most accurate. Marvel's comic stories were all made up, but they would keep true to the type of god that Heimdall was. The MCU would show off that Heimdall could see and hear across all nine realms, as he would often be tasked to get Thor out of trouble.

As for the dwarf and dark elves, the mystery was fleshed out by the MCU. In *Thor: Ragnarok*, the dwarves live in Nidavellir while in *Thor: The Dark World*, the dark elves live in Svartalfheim. This is interesting because the MCU is one of the few times that the dwarves and dark elves were classified as two different races inhabiting two separate worlds. They would also write that the dark elves were from Ginnungagap, which would be partially true since the worms that were found came from the creation times before day and night were made. Also, Eitri was the dwarf in *Ragnarök*, the same elf in Norse mythology that would make the mighty Mjölnir.

Ragnarok

This is a relatively new show that hit Netflix that tells a version of Norse mythology in a new way. The series follows a teenage boy named Magne who discovers he has special powers after his family moves to the mythical town of Edda, Norway. Edda, like those Eddas? This made it pretty obvious for the lovers of Norse mythology. We later learn that the giants that want to destroy the earth are still there in that town, which coincidentally is where Ragnarök took place during the Age of the Gods. The town itself has been subject to wild weather patterns, and the blame is put on the "evil" corporation, Jutul Industries.

Magne is based on Thor's son from mythology, Magni. The powers the teenager has lined up to that of the god himself. The Jutul family is based on Loki, and instead of ships and monsters, they own a corporation that is polluting the earth with toxins akin to the way the sea serpent did as he traveled to the area where Ragnarök would occur.

So, while it is a reimagining, it is a fairly accurate one. It is accurate in that it handles similar themes and ideas that show how these old myths are applicable today.

Game of Thrones/A Song of Ice and Fire

George R. R. Martin would base his book series on the classic *Ivanhoe*, but there is no doubt that he pulled from Norse mythology as well. The myths would also feed fan theories that tried to tie the events of the series to what had happened in Norse mythology.

The beginning of the television series would feature the infamous line, "Winter is coming." We know that the White Walkers are growing in numbers just outside the ice wall around Westeros, while the world is in the midst of war and chaos. The first connection would be the White Walkers to either the frost giants or to the army of Hel. While the brave warriors in Norse mythology would cross over to Valhalla, the others would find their way into the goddess's realm. The growing numbers of the White Walkers would best symbolize that. Also, the White Walkers were trying to cross the Wall, whereas the giants would cross the Bifrost on their way to Ragnarök.

Another tie to the Scandinavian belief in the days before Christianity was that time was cyclical, which means just as something can be destroyed, it could rise again. This is symbolic of the lasting winter in Westeros. Humanity in the series could have been on the brink of falling again as it had done during Ragnarök.

Another interesting thing is that the White Walkers would need to be killed with Valerian steel or dragon glass just as the giants would need to be killed with the weapons wielded by the gods. There were also plenty of nods to Norse mythology as the wolves, ravens, and dragons all played prominent roles in Martin's series.

Tolkien. Just Tolkien

J. R. R. Tolkien took a liking to Iceland. He was inspired by the landscape, the language, and Norse mythology. *The Hobbit* and *The Lord of the Rings* would go on to inspire other authors to add dwarves, elves, and other similar figures in their own works after the book increased in popularity. The novel series also inspired many of the themes of Led Zeppelin's music, which introduced an unknowing audience to references of Norse mythology. The *Völsunga Saga* was a childhood favorite, so what exactly did Tolkien take from the myths and the sagas when he wrote one of the most successful novel series in history?

First, the names of the dwarves from *The Hobbit* were almost identical to all the names found in Snorri's *Prose Edda*. This includes Gandalf, who also was named in Snorri's collection, but while Gandalf was a dwarf in mythology, his character model was none other than Odin. Gandalf was a traveler armed with a staff, and he would spread knowledge wherever he went, which is the same form that Odin would take as he went on his travels in disguise. Tolkien would also copy and paste the elves from the myths onto the pages of his own works.

Tolkien's favorite saga would also serve his narrative as well. We didn't cover the *Völsunga*

Saga in our book, but the narrative for it is about a dwarf Andvari who possesses a magical ring, the Andvaranaut, which was roughly based on Odin's ring Draupnir. Loki steals Anvari's ring, but the dwarf had cursed it to bring danger to anyone that had it. Loki gave the ring to the king who was immediately killed by the dragon Fafnir, and the dragon was killed thereafter by Sigurd. Not only was the ring from the saga the basis for the One Ring, but it was the rough idea of the story arc of *The Lord of the Rings*. We cannot forget the saga's dragon Fafnir, who became the model for Smaug. Both dragons were both in love with gold and would stop at nothing to get it.

Lastly, the setting of Middle Earth would tie to Midgard in Norse mythology, and the runes used in Tolkien's books were based on the Norse runes of mythology.

God of War

The popular video game series followed the god killer Kratos around as he vanquished all the gods of Greek mythology, but the 2018 game would see Kratos shift into the world of Norse mythology with their own take on events.

The first big wow moment is that the child in the game, Atreus, is Loki. Atreus is emotional and unpredictable, and Loki thrived on being unpredictable. Kratos and his wife Faye are his parents, but Faye's real name ends up being Laufey. In Norse mythology, Laufey and Farbauti are Loki's parents, and Farbauti is roughly translated to "cruel striker," which is exactly what Kratos is.

Jormungandr, the serpent that surrounded Midgard, appears in the game. Unlike in Norse mythology, the serpent is actually friendly and helps Kratos on his journey. You may remember that Jormungandr is actually Loki's son, but Atreus is still a child in the game. The game would lead you to believe that the serpent was from a different timeline after the battle with Thor sent him back to Kratos' age, so it could still very well be the son of Atreus.

Baldur does appear in-game as the chief antagonist. His portrayal is far different from the kind and loving god of the myths. During the story, it is revealed that Baldur sees his invulnerability as a curse. Perhaps if Loki had not killed Baldur in Norse mythology, having a gift that powerful would have driven Baldur insane. The game ends with Kratos and Atreus killing Baldur, which is going to be the spark that starts Ragnarök as the sequel's title suggests. In the myths, it is Loki and Hodr that kill Baldur, so the game still puts Loki at the center of the beloved god's death.

Freya is encountered during the game, and as she is assisting your characters, she reveals she was responsible for protecting her son Baldur. She was responsible for the "curse" Baldur carried because she was trying to protect him from his prophesied death. What makes this interesting is that this would suggest that Frigg and Freya are the same people, which, given the missing pieces of Norse mythology, it is completely plausible that they were the same.

Other appearances in the game: Mimir, who maintains his all-knowing nature, and Thor's sons, Modi, Magni, Hel, and Tyr. While Tyr is not really mentioned in Norse mythology, the game uses this to say that Tyr had aided the giants in the battle on Midgard. Odin imprisoned him or killed him because of his betrayal of the gods. Yes, in the game, gods are villains.

Assassin's Creed: Valhalla

Naturally, the name is a dead giveaway as it refers to the great hall where only the bravest warriors go after dying in battle. The references to Norse mythology wouldn't just stop at the name, though. While the gods have been portrayed as being "god-sized," *Valhalla* would give them their more human-like proportions.

In the poem "Lokasenna," Loki crashes into a party held by the gods. He then proceeds to insult each of the gods individually. This is given homage in the game by allowing you to engage with other Vikings and try to out-insult them.

While in a dream state, you find yourself in Asgard and fighting alongside the gods, but another place you actually visit in-game is Jotunheim. While there, you notice how cold it is, and that's because Jotunheim is in the midst of the winter of all winters.

The game feels more like a modern-day version of the sagas that were written about Norse mythology. The ultimate battle in the game is against the one and only Fenrir. Loki makes an appearance, and of course, is up to no good. The Allfather's spear Gungnir is a weapon you're given after completing the game the first time, and they even include rideable cats in an homage to Freya and her animal familiars.

Halo

The popular video game franchise offers many nods to Norse mythology throughout its games and its novel series. One of the first notable allusions to the myths is that Master Chief's armor is called the "MJOLNIR" armor.

Contact Harvest is one of the books based on the series, and in it, the residents of the planet Harvest are of Scandinavian descent. In the novel, there are two AI systems named Loki and Sif. Loki would shapeshift when he traded places with another AI system. Sif was the shipping operations AI, and in the book, Loki would destroy a driver that Sif would need and bring down the space elevators. The elevator strands were called "hairs." Once again, Loki was responsible for cutting off Sif's hair.

There were two seas named Munin and Hugin, which alluded to Odin's ravens. The farming machines were the Jotun of the novel. In the *Halo* universe, Spartans are the best and fiercest soldiers in the universe, and one specific group mentioned in the novel was named "Fireteam Fenrir."

Locations throughout the novel series and the video game series have been named after Norse gods such as Bifrost, Vigrond, Gladsheim, Ida (shortened version of Idavoll), and Mimir.

Valhalla and Ragnarök were both names of maps in the game's multiplayer mode.

In Norse mythology, Berserkers wore only bear or wolf skins as they would go into battle. Whether of their own volition or in a drug-induced state, they would lose sight of everything but vanquishing enemies, and they would attack anything in their path. This made them terrifying in the myths, and in the game, the Brutes would enter a berserker mode much like those followers of Odin.

Music

Led Zeppelin had more than a few hits based on the works of Tolkien, and we know how Tolkien used Norse mythology to inspire his novels. However, their hit "Immigrant Song" is a direct allusion to Thor.

While Motörhead would use the song "Deaf Forever" to use Norse mythology-inspired lyrics, it wasn't until 1988 when Swedish heavy metal band Bathory's album *Blood Fire Death* that a genre of heavy metal would be devoted to Vikings and Norse mythology. "Viking metal" would have a small following, but it was another Swedish band that made it "cool" to be a Viking.

Amon Amarth would easily take over the genre, and while the singer looks the part of a Viking, he is also an enthusiast of Norse mythology and the Viking Age. Besides being the frontman of the band, Johan Hegg co-owns Grimfrost, a company that makes contemporary clothing and authentic replicas of various Viking gear.

What About ______?

Again, if we listed every mention in pop culture of Norse mythology, we would have another book on our hands. The greatest aspect of having so much is knowing that the stories that began centuries ago still hold a special place with people today.

CONCLUSION

As you could see, some gods were filled out throughout Norse mythology and some were given hardly a mention. While it is frustrating as enthusiasts having to sell a character short, we can only work with what we are given. Even though we have reached the end and met the gods, there are still a few more surprises for you.

The first is how the Norse gods would find their way into something we use every week. Can't wait for Friday? Got a case of the Monday blues? You can thank the Norse gods six days of the week, then! Nordic names for the days of the week were actually derived from Latin, and even as the church would take over the lands, bits of Old Norse were left intact. So which gods got their own day?

- **Sunnudagr (Sunday):** Sól may have met an unfortunate end during Ragnarök, but she lives on Sunday.

- **Mánadagr (Monday):** Her brother, Mani, would get his own day as well. In Norse mythology, there were two distinctions of the moon. The first was the person Mani, and the other was the literal moon.

- **Tysdagr (Tuesday):** The Roman god of war was Mars, which translated over to Tyr, who was known in some instances as the god of justice and war.

- **Ódinsdagr (Wednesday):** Odin can be compared to the Roman god Mercury, so in Norse tradition, Odin (also called "Woden") would become the name for Wednesday.

- **Tórsdagr (Thursday):** Replace the "u" with the "o" and you get Thorsday. Thor would be known as Jupiter in Roman belief because both were gods of lightning and thunder.

- **Frjádagr (Friday):** Freya or Frigg would be associated with Venus as the goddess of love, and we all love Fridays!

- **Laugardagr (Saturday):** This is the only day that was not for a god except for the Latin god Saturn. Traditionally, this was the day of rest and bathing for the Vikings, which means they did not do much else. Also, yes, Vikings were actually a very hygienic people.

Getting to talk about the gods as we would to our friends and significant others is such a break from having to discuss them as a lecture from "Norse Mythology 101." Knowing that these centuries-old tales have to have a few of our own words really makes putting these books together worth it.

We got to learn just how these characters were preserved and why some have lapses or conflicting biographies. Thanks to those Eddas and the new Norse religions, we will surely never have to worry about losing them. We covered the bloody beginnings of creation, and now you can point to the clouds and say they all look like brains.

With apologies to Idun and Tyr for some lack of information, we got to learn about the key characters throughout Norse mythology. We also got to retell some of the best myths that surround them from the comical to the tragic.

Finally, the gods live on in modern culture, from the box office giants of the MCU to the video game worlds and music. There was still so much to cover, and there will most likely be even more tributes paid to the gods in the future.

What we hope you can take away from all this is a new or reinvigorated love for Norse mythology. Hearing the myths as more of a story as opposed to an off-putting YouTube video or unfulfilling book might make you want to take a deeper dive and maybe you can figure out the mystery of which worlds made up the nine or if Frigg and Freya were the same people. Maybe you could be the first to figure out more of Tyr's backstory. We are always searching for ourselves, and that's why we will continue to make more additions to History Brought Alive.

We said a couple of more additions to what we already covered. So we will leave you with

"Lessons from Odin."

- **Always Seek Wisdom:** As long as there is breath in your lungs, the quest for knowledge should never stop. Odin traveled constantly and would go to great lengths to get knowledge.

- **Have Trusted Advisors:** Odin learned things on his own, but Odin would turn to his ravens, the council of gods and goddesses, and Mimir. Having a circle built with people you trust will always keep you level-headed.

- **Listen To Others:** Even on his journey for knowledge, Odin would seek the words of the gods and goddesses, humans, nature and animals, the dead, and every other being in the nine realms. This is an aspect that many of us today cannot do. We can have a trusted circle, but we often shut down to any voices outside those walls. This is not a call to be harmonious and agree with all of those voices because that is unrealistic. Conflict is as sure as the sunrise. However, understanding all others around you will make your disagreements not appear to be from ignorance.

- **Master Your Words:** Odin was a poetic speaker, and should teach us that our words have power. You can accomplish more with a few words than any other method. You have the power to change and inspire, so speak, as Odin would.

- **Take Responsibility:** While Odin would rely on others, he never tried to pass the blame for the things he handled.

- **You Can't Change Fate, But You Can Change How You Face It:** Long lesson title, but the message should be there. Odin knew Ragnarök was coming and he tried to prevent it. However, even when he knew that the battle was coming, he faced it as bravely as he had everything else. Whatever happens in your life, bad or good, should all be faced bravely and with a certain elegance.

- **Wisdom Takes Sacrifice:** This doesn't mean gouging out the eye for knowledge, but anything worth truly learning will not come easy. Writers will research for a book for days, giving up time they could use writing or taking care of themselves. However, in order to have the knowledge to write that book, they needed to make the sacrifice. College students lose sleep and tuition money trying to gain knowledge. When that writer hands in a finished product or when that student graduates, sacrifices for knowledge are worth it.

Now, it is in your hands. Go forth and seek knowledge!

REFERENCES

Apel, T. (2021a, August 24). *Idun*. Mythopedia.
https://mythopedia.com/topics/idun

Apel, T. (2021b, November 3). *Freyr*. Mythopedia.
https://mythopedia.com/topics/freyr

Apel, T. (2021c, November 14). *Thor*. Mythopedia.
https://mythopedia.com/topics/thor

Apel, T. (2021d, November 18). *Baldur*. Mythopedia.
https://mythopedia.com/topics/baldur

Apel, T. (2021e, November 18). *Freya*. Mythopedia.
https://mythopedia.com/topics/freya

Apel, T. (2021f, November 18). *Frigg*. Mythopedia.
https://mythopedia.com/topics/frigg

Apel, T. (2021g, November 18). *Heimdall*. Mythopedia.
https://mythopedia.com/topics/heimda
ll

Apel, T. (2021h, November 18). *Loki*. Mythopedia.
https://mythopedia.com/topics/loki

Apel, T. (2021i, November 18). *Odin*.

Mythopedia.
https://mythopedia.com/topics/odin

Apel, T. (2021j, November 18). *Tyr*.
Mythopedia.
https://mythopedia.com/topics/tyr

Cat. (2018, June 8). *The Tale of Loki Bound
until the End of the World*. Asgard.
https://www.asgard.scot/blog/2018/06
/the-tale-of-loki-bound

Centre of Excellence. (2018, October 29). *A
Guide to Norse Gods and Goddesses*.
Centre of Excellence.
https://www.centreofexcellence.com/no
rse-gods-
goddesses/#:~:text=Odin%2C%20Frigg
%2C%20Thor%2C%20Loki

CliffsNotes. (2015). *Canto XXXIV*.
Cliffsnotes.com.
https://www.cliffsnotes.com/literature/
d/the-divine-comedy-inferno/summary-
and-analysis/canto-xxxiv

Guide to Iceland. (2013, January 24). *The
Ultimate Guide to Vikings and Norse
Gods in Iceland*. Guide to Iceland.
https://guidetoiceland.is/history-
culture/vikings-and-norse-gods-in-
iceland

Halopedia. (2022, March 19). *List of references
to Norse mythology in Halo*. Halopedia.

https://www.halopedia.org/List_of_ref
erences_to_Norse_mythology_in_Halo

Harlansson, K. (2004). *DragonBear History: All That: Eddas and Sagas.* Www.dragonbear.com. http://www.dragonbear.com/eddas.html

Jackson, J. (2021, December 14). *106 - Norse Myths 06 - Heimdall.* These Fantastic Worlds. https://thesefantasticworlds.com/106-norse-myths-06-heimdall/

James. (2011, May 18). *A Classic a Day: The Dwarven Wager.* A Classic a Day. http://aclassicaday.blogspot.com/2011/05/dwarven-wager.html#:~:text=Soon%20after%2C%20Brokk%20presented%20Loki

Juckiewicz, L. (2020, December 11). *Assassins Creed Valhalla: 10 Norse Mythology References You Might Have Missed.* TheGamer. https://www.thegamer.com/assassins-creed-valhalla-norse-mythology-references/#:~:text=The%20title%20of%20the%20latest

Mark, J. J. (2021, August 25). *Fenrir.* World History Encyclopedia. https://www.worldhistory.org/Fenrir/

Marqvardsen, G. (2010, August 8). *Myths - Agnar and Geirrod*. Www.fnar.no. https://www.fnar.no/Web_Gjermund/norsemyths/human_myth2.shtml

Marvel Cinematic Universe Wiki. (n.d.-a). *Dark Elves*. Marvel Cinematic Universe Wiki. https://marvelcinematicuniverse.fandom.com/wiki/Dark_Elves

Marvel Cinematic Universe Wiki. (n.d.-b). *Eitri*. Marvel Cinematic Universe Wiki. https://marvelcinematicuniverse.fandom.com/wiki/Eitri

Matier, D. (2019, October 21). *Norse Mythology: The Binding of Fenrir*. LetterPile. https://letterpile.com/creative-writing/Norse-Mythology-The-Binding-of-Fenrir

McCoy, D. (n.d.-a). *Hodr*. Norse Mythology for Smart People. https://norse-mythology.org/hodr/

McCoy, D. (n.d.-b). *The Kidnapping of Idun*. Norse Mythology for Smart People. https://norse-mythology.org/tales/the-kidnapping-of-idun/

McCoy, D. (n.d.-c). *Thor the Transvestite*. Norse Mythology for Smart People. https://norse-mythology.org/tales/thor-the-transvestite/

McCoy, D. (2012a). *The Death of Baldur - Norse Mythology for Smart People*. Norse Mythology for Smart People. https://norse-mythology.org/tales/the-death-of-baldur/

McCoy, D. (2012b). *The Mead of Poetry - Norse Mythology for Smart People*. Norse Mythology for Smart People. https://norse-mythology.org/tales/the-mead-of-poetry/

McCoy, D. (2016, June). *Gungnir*. Norse Mythology for Smart People. https://norse-mythology.org/gungnir/

Norman. (2012, May 15). *The War of the Aesir and Vanir*. The Norse Gods. https://thenorsegods.com/the-war-of-the-aesir-and-vanir/

Norman. (2013a, November 11). *The Death of Balder*. The Norse Gods. https://thenorsegods.com/the-death-of-balder/

Norman. (2013b, November 12). *Loki's Flyting*. The Norse Gods. https://thenorsegods.com/lokis-flyting/#:~:text=He%20called%20out%2C%20%E2%80%9CThe%20gods

Norman. (2013c, November 20). *Ragnarok*. The Norse Gods. https://thenorsegods.com/ragnarok/

Roua, V. (2017, July 23). *10 Influences From The Norse Mythology In J.R.R. Tolkien's Works.* The Dockyards. https://www.thedockyards.com/10-facts-j-r-r-tolkien-influenced-norse-culture/

Roxl, R. (2020, September 28). *10 Changes God Of War Made From Norse Mythology.* Game Rant. https://gamerant.com/god-of-war-changes-from-norse-mythology/

Scott, J. (2020, December 3). *A Beginner's Guide to Norse Mythology.* Life in Norway. https://www.lifeinnorway.net/norse-mythology/

Skjalden. (2011a, June 1). *Creation of the World in Norse Mythology.* Nordic Culture. https://skjalden.com/creation-of-the-world-in-norse-mythology/#

Skjalden. (2011b, June 1). *The Nine Realms in Norse Mythology.* Nordic Culture. https://skjalden.com/nine-realms-in-norse-mythology/

Skjalden. (2018, July 29). *Norse Sagas - Freyr and the giantess Gerd - Norse mythology.* Nordic Culture. https://skjalden.com/freyr-and-the-giantess-gerd/

Skjalden. (2020, August 6). *Skidbladnir - Norse*

mythology. Nordic Culture. https://skjalden.com/skidbladnir/

Sons of Vikings. (2019, April 17). *Game of Thrones and Norse Mythology*. Sons of Vikings. https://sonsofvikings.com/blogs/news/game-of-thrones-and-norse-mythology

Sons of Vikings. (2020, July 3). *Viking Lore: A Quick Intro to Norse Eddas and Sagas*. Sons of Vikings. https://sonsofvikings.com/blogs/history/viking-lore-a-quick-intro-to-norse-eddas-and-sagas

The Poetic Edda Index. (2019). Sacred-Texts.com. https://www.sacred-texts.com/neu/poe/index.htm

Travers, P. (2020, November 16). *Amon Amarth's Johan Hegg's Guide To Vikings*. Kerrang! https://www.kerrang.com/amon-amarths-johan-heggs-guide-to-vikings

Vali. (n.d.). *Myths and Folklore Wiki*. Retrieved March 27, 2022, from https://mythus.fandom.com/wiki/Vali#:~:text=In%20Norse%20mythology%2C%20V%C3%A1li%20is

Vaynshteyn, G. (2020, February 3). *The "Ragnarok" Mythology Primer You Need*. Www.refinery29.com.

https://www.refinery29.com/en-us/2020/02/9333645/what-is-ragnarok-netflix-based-on-norse-mythology

Viking Ship Museum. (n.d.). *The names of the weekdays.* Vikingeskibsmuseet I Roskilde. Retrieved April 2, 2022, from https://www.vikingeskibsmuseet.dk/en/professions/education/viking-age-people/the-names-of-the-weekdays#:~:text=In%20the%20Nordic%20countries%2C%20the

Visual, A. (2021, July 26). *Norse Mythology vs MCU. What's The Difference?* Geeks Gonna Geek. https://geeksgonnageek.com/norse-mythology-vs-mcu-whats-the-difference/

Wardruna.com - About Wardruna. (n.d.). Www.wardruna.com. Retrieved March 31, 2022, from https://www.wardruna.com/about/

Wigington, P. (2019, July 5). *What is the Asatru Pagan Tradition?* Learn Religions. https://www.learnreligions.com/asatru-modern-paganism-2562545

OTHER BOOKS BY HISTORY BROUGHT ALIVE

- Ancient Egypt: Discover Fascinating History, Mythology, Gods, Goddesses, Pharaohs, Pyramids, and More from the Mysterious Ancient Egyptian Civilization.

Available now on Kindle, Paperback, Hardcover & Audio in all regions

- Greek Mythology: Explore The Timeless Tales Of Ancient Greece, The Myths, History & Legends of The Gods, Goddesses, Titans, Heroes, Monsters & More

Available now on Kindle, Paperback, Hardcover & Audio in all regions

- Mythology for Kids: Explore Timeless Tales, Characters, History, & Legendary Stories from Around the World. Norse, Celtic, Roman, Greek, Egypt & Many More

Available now on Kindle, Paperback, Hardcover

& Audio in all regions

- Mythology of Mesopotamia: Fascinating Insights, Myths, Stories & History From The World's Most Ancient Civilization. Sumerian, Akkadian, Babylonian, Persian, Assyrian and More

Available now on Kindle, Paperback, Hardcover & Audio in all regions

- Norse Magic & Runes: A Guide To The Magic, Rituals, Spells & Meanings of Norse Magick, Mythology & Reading The Elder Futhark Runes

Available now on Kindle, Paperback, Hardcover & Audio in all regions

- Norse Mythology, Vikings, Magic & Runes: Stories, Legends & Timeless Tales From Norse & Viking Folklore + A Guide To The Rituals, Spells & Meanings of Norse Magick & The Elder Futhark Runes. (3 books in 1)

Available now on Kindle, Paperback, Hardcover & Audio in all regions

- Norse Mythology: Captivating Stories & Timeless Tales Of Norse Folklore. The Myths, Sagas & Legends of The Gods,

Immortals, Magical Creatures, Vikings & More

Available now on Kindle, Paperback, Hardcover & Audio in all regions

- Norse Mythology for Kids: Legendary Stories, Quests & Timeless Tales from Norse Folklore. The Myths, Sagas & Epics of the Gods, Immortals, Magic Creatures, Vikings & More

Available now on Kindle, Paperback, Hardcover & Audio in all regions

- Roman Empire: Rise & The Fall. Explore The History, Mythology, Legends, Epic Battles & Lives Of The Emperors, Legions, Heroes, Gladiators & More

Available now on Kindle, Paperback, Hardcover & Audio in all regions

- The Vikings: Who Were The Vikings? Enter The Viking Age & Discover The Facts, Sagas, Norse Mythology, Legends, Battles & More

Available now on Kindle, Paperback, Hardcover & Audio in all regions

FREE BONUS FROM HBA: EBOOK BUNDLE

Greetings!

First of all, thank you for reading our books. As fellow passionate readers of History and Mythology, we aim to create the very best books for our readers.

Now, we invite you to join our VIP list. As a welcome gift, we offer the History & Mythology Ebook Bundle below for free. Plus you can be the first to receive new books and exclusives! Remember it's 100% free to join.

Scan the QR code to join.

<u>Keep up to date with us on:</u>

YouTube: History Brought Alive

Facebook: History Brought Alive

www.historybroughtalive.com